ODIN'S PROMISE

Sandy Brehl

CRISPIN BOOKS

Crispin Books is an imprint of Crickhollow Books, based in Milwaukee, Wisconsin. Together, Crispin and Crickhollow publish a variety of fiction and nonfiction for discerning readers.

Our titles are available from your favorite bookstore online or around the corner. For a complete catalog of all our titles or to place special orders (for classroom use, etc.):

www.CrispinBooks.com

www.CrickhollowBooks.com

Odin's Promise
© 2014, Sandra Brehl

ISBN-13: 978-1-883953-65-2
(ISBN-10: 1-883953-65-0)

Juvenile Fiction / Historical / World War II
Family & Friends / Action & Adventure / Middle-Grade Novel

First Crispin Books Edition
Cover illustration by Kathleen Spale (www.KathleenSpale.com)

To the original Odin
and to Dondi, Jenny, Bjorn, and Kaffe.
Your love and strength will never leave me.

For more about the writing and topics of
Odin's Promise,
visit:
www.SandyBrehl.com

For a glossary of Norwegian & German words
that appear in the story,
see p. 229.

Contents

Chapter One

A Mountain of Fear

Ytre Arna, Norway
August, 1940

Mari popped a wild raspberry into her mouth, then wiped the red juice from her fingers on the grass. She tossed her long brown braid over her shoulder, picked up her basket of berries, and began making her way back to the path.

"Come, Odin," she called. "Time to go home. Leave some rabbits for next time."

Odin rarely needed a second shout, even in the heat of a chase. This time, though, he was riveted on the mountain trail, staring intently into the nearby treeline, thick with shadows and pines. What had gotten into him? Ever since Papa had tucked Odin in her arms three years ago on her eighth birthday, when he wasn't much larger than a rabbit himself, he had been her constant companion. He followed her bidding before he was old enough for training, and now, as large as he was, he did whatever she said, even if her command was given in a whisper.

This time he didn't budge, didn't even seem to hear her.

As Mari neared the path, she noticed rustling in the trees. Low pine branches swayed, and something substantial was shuffling through the dried needles on the forest floor, heading toward the trail. She reached for the scruff of Odin's neck and buried her fingers in the bristled fur of his raised hackles.

"Come, boy, we're not here to hunt," she whispered firmly, tugging at his neck. It was late August, so bears had been seen along the mountainsides, usually gorging themselves on ripe berries.

But Odin's Norwegian elkhound instincts were on full alert, and Mari anticipated a bark was ready to spring from his black throat at any moment.

"No, Odin." She spoke quietly but firmly, and tugged again, this time trying to drag them both away from the berry brambles and down the open slope. "Let's go home."

That's when she heard voices speaking—in German.

Her already racing heartbeat escalated, thumping against her ribs. She bent lower and wrapped her arms around Odin's powerful neck and shoulders, trying to drag him away from the trail that headed back down the mountain to the village below. Maybe they should stay out of sight, she thought.

Maybe it wasn't a bear. Maybe it was something she

feared more. *German soldiers.* They were everywhere in her village, and were said to patrol the mountain trails too, looking for suspicious activity.

But Odin wouldn't budge. The black elkhound dug in, rooted to the spot, as steady and solid as a boulder. His lips curled back from his teeth. She heard a low rumble deep in his chest, a sound she had never heard from him before.

Odin's stare was locked on the treeline as two soldiers emerged. Both had their sidearms drawn, and one of the two was pointing his handgun at a third figure: Mr. Meier, her neighbor from the village. He stumbled ahead of the two Germans. Mari realized with a shock he had his hands tied behind his back.

Odin growled, then quieted to that rumble deep in his throat and chest. His lips pulled back even further in a snarl. Mari buried her face in the coarse scruff of his neck and gasped, realizing they would be seen.

When she lifted her head she saw that the second soldier was stopped on the trail just a few meters away from her, his gun aimed straight at Odin.

She recognized him right away. This pair of soldiers often patrolled together in Ytre Arne, and they had nicknames among the villagers. It was "Scarecrow" who faced her with the gun, a tall, scrawny soldier who seemed impossibly loose-limbed and lanky. Mari had seen him goose-stepping in formation and wondered how he kept from tripping over his own feet. His thick blond hair stuck out from under the back of his cap like straw.

The other soldier, the short one, was "The Rat." His dark bristly mustache and muddy brown eyes were unexpected, since most of the German soldiers were blonde and fair, typical of the "superior" race Hitler so admired. The Rat kept his gun pointed at Mr. Meier's head. As the villager paused, The Rat shoved him in the back, causing the old man to stagger and fall to his knees.

"On your feet, stupid Jew!"

Odin's rumble deepened, building toward a growl, but Mari stroked his side and tried to quiet him.

Mr. Meier leaned on his elbow and scrambled to his feet. When he limped forward Mari saw blood flowing from his knee, soaking his ripped pants. Blood also trickled down the side of his face from a cut near his eye, spreading across his reddened, swelling cheek. Her gut twisted, and she clutched at Odin's fur to stop the trembling in her hands.

"Move," The Rat ordered, nudging the gun's muzzle into her neighbor's back. He muttered in German to Scarecrow with a jerk of his head toward Mari and her dog, "Find out what they're doing here, and then bring the pack."

Speaking German was no challenge for Mari, or for most Norwegians her age and older, but she followed the lead of her family and neighbors, pretending not to understand. It was the least they could do to show respect for their exiled King Haakon. She usually felt a smug satisfaction in forcing the occupiers to use Norwegian, watching them stammer and struggle for words at times.

Now it was she who was struggling, for breath, not words.

She tightened her hug, pressing herself into Odin's side. Her body trembled uncontrollably against Odin's rock-solid stance.

Scarecrow took a step toward them. "Up, *Fräulein,*" he commanded. His voice was thin and high. He looked young, barely older than her brother Bjorn. Yet his German uniform and boots showed wear, and his stance showed he meant what he said.

Mari jumped to her feet, holding onto Odin's neck as much for support as to control him. She wanted desperately to turn and run, but imagined being shot in the back. Instead she edged backward ever so slightly, pulling Odin with her. The loose stones of the trail shifted under her feet, her knees felt like noodles, and she struggled to stay upright.

"Why are you here? Is this man a friend of yours? Do you know him?" The Rat had paused on the trail, his eyes flicking back and forth from the young Norwegian girl to her growling black dog.

Mari looked at Mr. Meier's face, saw him drop his eyes and turn away from her with a slight shake of his head. Her throat was so tight she could barely breathe and her mouth was as cottony as a lark's nest. She opened her mouth, closed it again, and felt her eyes fill with tears.

"Answer me. Now. Do you know him? What are you

doing here?" Scarecrow's voice sounded as harsh as The Rat's, but his face looked less fierce. Whatever his expression meant, she couldn't stand looking at him. Her eyes focused on Odin's neck and she swallowed hard.

"He's . . . he's . . . I was picking berries. My basket is just over there." Her voice was barely audible, and she was certain she'd collapse if not for leaning on Odin. Her eyes darted first to the soldier's boots, then down the mountain toward home. The Rat was moving downhill, prodding Mr. Meier ahead of him on the trail, away from the open area of the raspberry thicket into the darkness of the pine woods. They disappeared quickly from sight.

"I'll go get my berry basket and go home now, *ja?*" The words burned when she spoke as acid rose in the back of her throat.

"That dog of yours will get himself shot, and you with him, if you can't control him. Think about that before you come sneaking around in the mountains again," Scarecrow snapped, waving his gun toward the ring of rocky crests surrounding her small village. She noticed that he looked anxiously down the trail. He seemed nervous to be left on his own to deal with her.

"Gather your things and go home—now. And if you have a brain in your head, you'll think twice about where you go and what you tell people about this."

He holstered his gun, slung a large heavy pack over his shoulder, and turned to follow the other two men.

Mari wasted no time scooting back toward the wild raspberry patch. She kept one hand on Odin's neck, murmuring reassurances as much to herself as to him. Not far from the path, she nudged Odin into a small stand of trees, listening intently. She could still hear the heels of distant boots digging into skittering stones on the trail.

"Sit, Odin, *shhh*. They're walking toward the village, probably going to their headquarters. Even though Mama will worry about how late we are, we'll wait here until we're sure they're gone."

She settled on the mossy ground and Odin lay beside her, resting his head in her lap. She struggled for breath as if she had run a race. She stroked the dog's dark fur.

"I was so afraid, my heart is still pounding. But you—you were ready to fight them both, weren't you, my Viking warrior." She leaned in close and kissed his snout, rubbing the velvety inside of his ear.

"Don't ever do that again, Odin," she scolded. "I wouldn't survive without you."

He lifted his head and licked her face.

"I'm taking that as a promise," she said.

When ten minutes passed with nothing more to observe than gulls flying high overhead, a lonely thrush in the bushes, and a few butterflies dancing about, Mari retrieved her basket and started down the mountain path. Odin seemed aware of his promise and never strayed more than a few steps away from her side.

Since the start of the surprise German occupation of Norway in April of that year, Mari had seen plenty of soldiers. Too many soldiers, too many green uniforms with swastikas, too many tall black boots.

And too many guns.

Now she hated the Germans, even though they claimed to be friendly. Posters plastered all over the village proclaimed Hitler's soldiers were like Vikings, that they shared a "superior" race, destined to rule the world. Posters were everywhere, new ones appearing all the time. She often found herself walking with her eyes downcast to avoid them.

Norwegian resistance might have been more successful if leaders like Quisling hadn't welcomed the Nazis in order to gain power and favor in their eyes. That just made it easier for the Germans to pretend they were invited into her homeland, not occupying it by force. The things she had seen and heard in only a few months made it perfectly clear who was in control in Norway now, a country with many good harbors on the North Sea, not so far from England.

But nothing she had seen or heard in the last four months had prepared her for what she had just witnessed on the mountainside.

As she and Odin neared the edge of town, Mari scanned the surroundings for any sign of the soldiers. Mr. Meier's home was on the downhill side of the road, just across from her front gate on the outskirts of Ytre Arna.

The village was not a large one, and everyone knew each other well. She had known Mr. Meier as a friendly neighbor since she was a small child.

She stooped down on the trail and set the berry basket down, pulling Odin close. Her eyes searched every inch of Mr. Meier's yard, his closed door, then beyond to the shed in back and the rocky steps down to the fjord. If birds sang or gulls cried she didn't hear them, so focused was she on listening for any faint sound of stomping boots or German commands.

There was no sign of movement, no indication that Mr. Meier or the soldiers were in the area.

When Odin squirmed in her arms, she stood. The sun bounced off the sapphire waters just beyond her neighbor's red-tiled roof, and she shaded her eyes. Her knees were stiff when she rose to continue the short distance home. She rolled her tense and aching shoulders, then forced her feet to move.

"Come, Odin," she whispered, releasing her fingers from her tight grip on the fur of his shoulders. "Mama will be upset that we're late. It's probably best not to tell her about this."

She picked up the basket and hurried toward the safety of her own yard.

Chapter Two

Safe At Home

Mari was surprised to see her mother waiting for her, watching from the back stoop. Before she had even reached the yard, Mama had unlatched the gate and met her on the road.

"What happened, where have you been so long?" Mama's eyes were red, her voice trembled. She clutched her daughter's shoulders, examined her face, and then hugged her fiercely.

"Mama, stop, you're spilling the berries!" Mari squirmed loose of the hug, surprised by this unexpected greeting.

Her mother wrapped an arm around her waist and nearly dragged Mari through the gate. "Hurry, little one, let's get inside." She turned to latch it, then leaned over the fence and craned her neck to look down the road toward town before returning to Mari's side.

Mama's worried face, her behavior and tone, were so

unlike her steady, matter-of-fact nature. It shook loose Mari's memory of the recent strange encounter up in the hills, and she felt her gut twist and churn.

"Mama . . ." Suddenly Mari felt a little light-headed, her knees buckled a little and she dropped her berry basket on the ground. Some of the raspberries tipped out onto the stone path.

Mama took one look at her. "Are you all right, little one?" She checked Mari's arms and head, turning her this way and that in search of injuries. Mari slumped into Mama's hug.

Odin pressed against them both, whining slightly and licking Mari's arm.

Mari felt the press of a kiss on the top of her head. She sucked at the air, trying to take a deep breath, and swallowed hard several times before she could speak. She looked up into Mama's face and managed to say, "I'm fine. I just need to sit down."

Her mother slid her arm around Mari's waist, then led them to the garden bench. Odin circled them repeatedly, reached up to lick Mari's face, and eventually rested his head on her lap. Her hand instantly reached for him and stroked his ear.

She felt Mama brush loose strands of hair off her face and cradle the back of her head as if she were still a baby. They sat together, rocking slightly, until they were both breathing more normally again.

"That's my baby girl. Slowly, now, tell me why you are

late, what made you sick. You were as white as a sheet."

Mari managed to report what she had witnessed, interrupted a few times as she had to pause to fight back tears. Mama's rocking and patting kept pace with the story.

When Mari stopped, Mama leaned closer to her and whispered, "You're sure it was Mr. Meier?"

"Of course I'm sure! He was as near to me as the kitchen door! But I didn't help him, or even speak to him. When they asked if I knew him, I didn't answer. I was too afraid."

"Shh, keep your voice quiet," Mama said. "We should go inside now." Mari saw her mother scan the mountain path and the road into the village.

Mari pulled herself to her feet and swiped at the corners of her eyes.

"First I'll see if I can save some of these berries, Mama," Mari said, picking up her basket and kneeling in the grass. Instead of spilled berries, though, she found wet streaks of purple-red trampled into the stone walk and grass. "They're ruined! All those beautiful raspberries wasted! Now you won't have enough for Papa's birthday surprise."

Mama pulled her to her feet and turned her toward the house. "We'll make do with what we have. We're getting to be pretty good at making do, don't you agree, little one? Wasted berries are not worth your worry. We'll find a way to make something good out of this trouble." She handed Mari her basket, looking over her shoulder again.

"Let's get started. Papa will be home soon. Leave your

shoes at the door, I don't want juice stains on my clean floors."

Mari nodded and untied her shoes. She set them on the stoop to clean later. She snatched at Odin's neck as he tried to push past her. "Oh, no, my hero. Your feet are messy, too, but you can't leave them by the door."

Odin sat at her side and lifted a paw into her hand. He enjoyed having Mari's face at eye level and took full advantage of the chance to lick away her dried salty tears. His whiskers tickled her ear and she laughed, wiping each paw tenderly.

Odin's entire coat was as glossy black as a raven's head, except for the toes of each front paw and the tip of his tail, the only spots that were snowy white. Or at least were white when he was clean. Often these bits of fur were stained green from grass or brown from creek mud.

Now, even though Mari fetched some soapy water and scrubbed away, the red stain of crushed berries clung to his fur.

She looked toward the path and saw the spotted pebbles, the streaked grass. Mr. Meier's bloody knee and face, the blood-streaked trail where he had fallen, those images flashed into her mind. She swallowed hard. Should she have done something different to help the old man?

"Mari, I need your help," Mama called, snapping her back to the present, safe at home with her family. That's when Mari noticed that waxwings were settling in to feast on the scattered crushed berries. Maybe something good could come from trouble. Maybe.

She honestly couldn't image any good would come from the Germans taking over her homeland. Marching Mr. Meier away bleeding, at gunpoint, was certainly not something good.

Chapter Three

Secrets On the Stairs

By the time Papa's birthday dinner was over, Mari stopped thinking about Mr. Meier and the soldiers. Mama had worked her magic in the kitchen, creating a meal that included at least bits and pieces of all of Papa's favorites despite the shortages. She had even served butter, to Papa's delight.

After the invasion of the Germans, all the parks and flowerbeds in town had been converted to vegetable gardens that summer, the precious land shared by the entire village. Mari enjoyed working on a small plot her family planted, either on her own or with her grandma. Most of their small share of the harvest would be dried, pickled, or preserved to help survive winter rationing. Since the Germans had arrived, the stores no longer sold many of the foods they had stocked before the war.

Mari knew that Mama had been planning this meal for a long time, gleaning and hoarding supplies, trading small favors with neighbors for extras from time to time. For weeks Mari watched her barter for enough butter to add to the potatoes and fresh beans she served on Papa's birthday. There was even a bit of butter to dab on the lefsa. Topped with wild raspberries, no one seemed to miss sugar and cinnamon. Mari sipped and savored as they each enjoyed one small cup of *real* coffee with dessert, just for this occasion.

There was actually enough food so that her mother smiled and nodded when Mari asked if Odin could celebrate too, with a bite of bread and gravy.

"Sonja, you have made this another very memorable birthday," Papa said. He reached past Mari's older brother Bjorn and their grandma to pat his wife's hand. "*Tusen takk* to you all for such a happy celebration, and for your love. If only Lise could be here. But she is well, and knows she is loved. We are all truly blessed."

Papa reached for Mari's hand and lifted it to his lips, bowing like a gentleman at a fancy ball. "And thank you, baby girl, for providing these berries for dessert, my favorite!" He kissed her cheek, then beamed at his family.

Mari grinned when she watched his finger slide along the edge of his plate. Papa licked the last of the juice from his finger, tinting the tips of his grey mustache pink.

Mama reached for his plate and clucked her tongue, but couldn't hide her smile.

"Don't begrudge him that last lick, Sonja. Who knows what he'll be eating next year on his birthday."

Her grandma patted Papa's cheek and grinned at him. She laughed, "He always did enjoy his desserts, to the last morsel."

"I gathered enough berries for Mama to make him a cobbler, if it hadn't been for the trouble," Mari said.

"In times like these, we all need to share, baby girl. Don't look so worried about spilling some in the yard. It made me smile to see the birds enjoying their dinner, too."

"No, Papa, I mean the troub—"

Mama jumped up and began gathering dishes. "Mari, that will wait. Help me clear the table."

Mari wanted to sit and enjoy this family time, to pretend just a while longer that everything was normal. "Can't it wait, Mama?"

Then she noticed the look on her mother's face. To her surprise, even Bjorn and Bestemor Dagmar stood and helped clear the table. Mari stepped back a moment and watched as Papa gave Mama a questioning look. Mari saw Mama's forehead crease as she shook her head ever so slightly at him. Her brother and grandma worked without chatter or teasing, which was even more unusual.

In only a few minutes Mari had shaken the tablecloth outside the kitchen door and folded it neatly for a future event. Bjorn and her grandma were again seated at the table. When Mari pulled out her own chair to join them, she felt Mama tug her hand.

"Come, little one, you've had a very long day. Let's get you into bed."

"No, Mama, please. It's still early and Papa is hardly ever home in time for dinner these days. I want to stay and tell him about Mr. Meier."

Mama held her hand and led her to the table, shaking her head at another of his puzzled looks. "Give Papa a good-night birthday kiss and do as you are told. I'll need your help tomorrow. You're exhausted."

"But—"

"I'll tell him all about it for you. Now take Odin and get yourself ready for bed. I'll be up later to tell you a story." Mari felt herself being dragged to the stairs, and she heard in Mama's voice that she meant business. After looking over her shoulder and seeing them all seated and watching her, she turned back to the steps and started up to bed.

Odin followed her to the top and then led the way into her room, but Mari stopped and tiptoed back down to the landing. She paused in the shadows, just before the stairway turned to the kitchen. Careful not to make a sound, she sat down on a step and leaned against the wall, straining to hear their voices. Only the clinking of cups and saucers and the sounds of dishes being washed met her ear, but she refused to give up yet.

Ever since she could remember she had been easily frightened. Almost anything from a loud noise to meeting people she didn't know could give her the shivers, and sometimes even left her half sick. She didn't mind in the least being "baby girl" or "little one" at those times. She was the youngest of her classmates, some of whom had already turned twelve.

As a late-life surprise for Mama and Papa, an unexpected addition, she was ten years younger than Bjorn and twelve years younger than her sister Lise. It was as if she had been raised with five parents, since grandma—Bestemor—lived in a cottage at the back of their yard. She rather enjoyed being babied and found comfort in being watched over and worried about by all of them.

Mari felt a warm furry body lean into her. Odin had also crept down the steps to sit beside her. Her fingers slipped into his fur and massaged his neck. She had sat on this step just out of sight often in recent months, finding ways to overhear the scary details about the world that her parents discussed quietly when they thought she was in bed. And conversations about bad news were more and more frequent these days. That's the way she learned for sure that Germany's "occupation" of Norway was really an invasion, that Germans were not the friends they claimed to be, regardless of how they acted or what it said on the posters.

If it meant being left out of knowing what was happening in her village to her friends and neighbors, to her own family, she was tired of being "baby girl." After the invasion in April, she put her foot down and told Mama and Papa about the things she was learning in school. The Germans closed the school in early May, but Mr. Jensen had made the most of the last weeks they had together.

They had studied maps, even learned about Germany's

surprise invasion of Poland the year before. Then, in April, they shared news of the battles in Norway, when the Germans sailed into the harbors with their troops and took control of the airports and ports. They learned of King Haakon's escape to England with much of the ministry, treasury, and navy. Mari's work in school was always excellent, and she was credited with completing Year Five. All sixteen students in her class would move up to Year Six together in September.

After that, her parents agreed to include her in important discussions. But all too often they still shuffled her off to bed or on an errand while they discussed the latest news without her.

Maybe they were all going to bed soon themselves. She slid her hand from Odin's neck and leaned on the step, shifting slightly. She tried to get up without pressing on the squeaky spot. Then she heard Papa clear his throat. She froze, pressing her back into the wall and her hands into Odin's fur.

"So tell me what happened to Mr. Meier, and how was our Mari involved?"

Chapter Four

Bedtime Story

Mari pulled Odin's long warm body against her, caressing his ear. She had listened on the landing as long as she could stand it before crawling into bed. Kitchen talk continued from below, but that wasn't what was keeping her awake now. Her thoughts kept swirling, sorting and shuffling scenes from her mountain encounter, adding to that the details she had just heard.

"Sweet Odin, what would I do without you and your silky ears?" She lifted the ear she'd been stroking and kissed it. Odin shifted slightly, heaved a deep sigh, and began to snore, a sound that often soothed her to sleep like a lullaby.

Not this time. She slipped her arm out from under his head and moved to the window, lifting the blackout curtain ever so slightly.

The words from her family played out the ugly truth. Mr. Meier had been taken to the prison camp not far the German headquarters.

She was aware that radios were outlawed and most of the ones in the village had been confiscated just a few weeks earlier. Those who joined the Norwegian Nazi party, Quisling's NS, were permitted to keep radios and could listen to approved news broadcasts, but everyone else was required to turn theirs in. Some villagers even joined Quisling's party just to keep a radio. But a few others kept their radios, making sure the devices were well hidden, and tuned in to listen to the nightly British news, the BBC, in secret. News spread in whispered conversations through the village about the King or the state of the Allied forces and the war. Mari knew this was happening, but had no idea who was doing it. She just knew that her family always seemed to know more than she did.

Mari thought about Mr. Jensen and how openly he shared news and his feelings about the invasion with her class. She and the other school children had learned almost immediately to keep secrets, to avoid discussing any news or questions beyond the safety of their classroom and their own homes.

She was shocked to hear Papa report that someone had turned Mr. Meier in for hiding a radio. Somehow he had received warning that a patrol was coming for him. When the soldiers arrived to search his home and arrest him, the old man was on his way up the mountain. He was trying to take the radio to his cousins in Norheimsund.

The scene at the trail played out before her eyes over and over. The radio must have been in the heavy pack. She was ashamed that she hadn't spoken up for him, but what if she had? Would they have taken her to prison camp, too?

In most cases when people were found with radios there was a steep fine and perhaps a day or two of interrogation at headquarters.

But Mr. Meier was Jewish. The Nazis hated Jews. As a Jew, Mr. Meier would be lucky if they never released him from the prison camp. He would fare better there than if he were sent to a work camp in Germany.

Someone, Papa said, most likely one of their own neighbors, had turned him in.

Mr. Meier, a scrawny, half-bald old bachelor, always had a smile for Mari, and often a riddle. His garden had the most beautiful roses, even finer than Bestemor's. He also made fine jewelry and silver pieces, the best in the district.

Standing in her room at the window, she peeked out through the slight gap in the lifted curtain and stared across the path. Her house sat on a flat lot cut into the side of the mountain, with windows facing the road and the fjord. Mr. Meier's tiled roof stretched below her.

Someone she knew, someone she probably saw every day, had reported him. But who would do that?

Papa's words replayed over and over in her head: "We can't trust anyone. Too many are swallowing the propaganda. Some folks will do anything to please the Germans."

"Or to get extra ration cards and better paying jobs." The sharpness in her grandma's voice was so unfamiliar that at first Mari had not even known who was speaking. "If headquarters weren't on the opposite side of the village, German officers would be moving into Mr. Meier's home. I wonder how long it will take for some NS party member to move in as payback for other traitorous favors."

Mari stood staring at the fjord and lost track of time. She couldn't get the image of Mr. Meier's bloody face out of her mind.

The creak of footsteps on the stairs brought her back to her senses, and she slid back into bed. When the door opened, she closed her eyes and tried to match the rhythm of her breathing to Odin's. The smell of lavender told her it was her grandma. She felt the sheet being tugged up and over her shoulder. When Bestemor leaned in to kiss her cheek, Mari swung her arms around her neck and whimpered.

"Shh, my poor little thing."

Mari clung to her neck, her panicked breathing slowing in the safety of Bestemor's rocking arms.

"You should have been asleep hours ago."

Odin stood and stretched on the bed, as if agreeing with Bestemor. He circled several times on the bed, swishing them both in the face with his tail. Eventually he curled up again with a deep sigh.

By the time all three were settled, giggles had replaced Mari's whimpers.

"That's my girl. A little love and laughter calms the nerves, even on a day such as this. Maybe a story will help you sleep."

Mari curled her legs and slid down into bed, pulling her pillow onto Grandma's ample lap.

"That's my girl. I know a story that always makes you laugh, the story of the Emperor's New Clothes!"

Mari grinned and began telling the story herself.

The Emperor was so vain, so greedy that he was easily tricked. He was gullible and believed the stories the tailors told him about the beautiful new clothes they were weaving and stitching. The truth was right there in the mirror, but he was afraid he'd sound foolish if he admitted there were no clothes to admire, that the tailors were just waving their arms back and forth, pretending to make clothes that were invisible to the eye. But everyone in court was too afraid to speak the truth, to the Emperor or to the tailors.

Mari's favorite part was the parade. When the Emperor marched through the kingdom as naked as a lumbering bear, people were too afraid of his power to laugh or ask questions. Then one little boy spoke up. He called out that the Emperor was not wearing anything at all. Only then did the others, one by one, including finally the Emperor, recognize their own foolishness and admit the truth.

"Shh," Grandma whispered. "Let me finish so you can close your eyes and sleep."

Mari loved the feel of Grandma's thumb and fingers rubbing her earlobe. Maybe that's why Mari rubbed Odin's ears whenever she was upset. She snuggled deeper into her pillow and mumbled, "That's the end of the story,

Bestemor."

"I have a little more to add tonight, just listen."

Her grandma's voice was soft and lilting. Even though Mari had her eyes closed, she could tell Bestemor was smiling. "The Christmas nisse always know what goes on in secret, right? That's how they make sure good girls and boys get chocolate at Christmas and troublemakers get clods of mud—or worse."

"Mmm-hmm."

Grandma continued. "You've seen many of your schoolmates wearing nisse caps, even in summer, to show their contempt for the Germans and their solidarity as Norwegians? How could red knit caps hurt anyone, you must wonder, especially the 'superman' Germans?

"That's a good question to ask. And the answer is in your story. Even the slightest symbols or defiance make the Nazis nervous. They know their beliefs are based on lies, that they aren't *really* superior to anyone else, no matter how many ways they repeat it or how many posters they plaster on our walls. What they fear most is that they may not be able to fool everyone. They are afraid of anyone saying or doing anything to question their power. And so they put notices in the newspapers and on their posters, they forbid radios, they even make up ridiculous rules that nisse caps are *VERBOTTEN*, right?

"And that is why so many children are now wearing nisse caps, even on warm days. Just like the little boy who told the truth, our children will remind them that we see the truth, that lies won't last. Since the Germans claim to be friends, they won't snatch the caps off the heads of our children!"

Grandma chuckled softly, then stroked Mari's head, tucking strands of hair behind her ear. "Understand, baby girl?"

"Mmm-hmm," Mari mumbled before sinking into sleep.

Chapter Five

Odin in Danger

"Good boy, nice catch!"

Mari picked up the knotted driftwood Odin dropped at her feet and rubbed his neck. She pretended to throw it toward the mountain trail, then spun in place and released it down the village road. Odin anticipated her toss and did a pebble-spraying turn as she released the stick. He took off toward the village and charged around the bend in the road.

When he didn't return immediately, she pictured him getting some friendly attention from someone on the street. Her grin disappeared when she heard him barking loudly, sounding frantic.

Mari raced down the road, stretching her arms wide at the turn to slow herself. As she rounded the corner she slammed into the uniformed back of Scarecrow. He stumbled, spread his boots wide and grabbed her arm to steady them both.

The Rat was holding Odin's stick high out of reach, sneering and taunting him. Odin stood rigidly, front paws planted and pressing tensed muscles back into his haunches. He lunged forward with each sharp bark, not the playful kind Mari heard when Bjorn teased with a toy.

"Odin, sit!" she shouted, causing both the dog's and the German soldier's heads to snap in her direction. Odin turned and lunged toward Scarecrow, who dropped Mari's arm and put his hand on his pistol.

"Sit, Odin. Stay!" she commanded, stepping forward and kneeling into his chest. Odin immediately dropped into a sit, but his hackles were raised and his lips curled back. His barking stopped, but the low rumble deep in his throat and chest made her fingers tingle.

Mari looked over her shoulder at the soldiers. The Rat's sneer was still in place, but Scarecrow's face began to relax, the corners of his mouth twitching slightly. She breathed a sigh of relief when she saw that his hand had dropped back to his side.

"*Der dummkopf hund*!" The Rat shouted. "Your stupid dog doesn't know how to play our little game! You'd best keep him at home if you don't want to find him dead in the road with a bullet in his head!"

Mari's anger at the threat overcame her fear. "Of course he knows how to play. He's not stupid! He wouldn't even bark at you if you hadn't grabbed his toy and teased him. You don't know anything about dogs, do you?"

She felt Odin respond to her angry voice. His back

legs tensed, the way they did when he spotted a rabbit or knew a toy was about to be tossed. Mari pressed his rump back to the ground, and whispered in his ear, "Sit."

The Rat glared and pointed at the two of them with the driftwood stick. Before he spoke, he glanced at nearby shoppers on the street and faces peeking out through storefronts. When he spoke his voice was quieter, but his teeth were clenched nearly as much as Odin's.

"If your dog is so smart why does he keep turning up where he doesn't belong? And you are always with him, aren't you? I advise you to stay home. And train him to obey."

Mari's stomach twisted and she fought her natural response to duck her head and agree. She was shocked to find herself looking straight into his cold eyes, returning his glare. "Odin obeys *me* just fine. Since when do we not belong in our own village streets? Or on our own mountainside, for that matter?"

There was a silence. Mari thought everyone on the street were frozen in place. Scarecrow, who had not spoken until then, cleared his throat . "He's a beautiful dog, don't you think, Hans? Such a thick coat." He stepped between Mari and The Rat, holding his open hand in front of Odin's mouth, palm up.

Mari patted Odin and spoke softly near his ear, "Give paw, Odin."

Scarecrow's face lit up when Odin placed a paw firmly in his hand. The soldier shook it lightly, released it, then reached under Odin's chin and rubbed. He looked back at The Rat and said, "You see, Hans, he just wanted his stick. He's being a good guard dog for this little *Fräulein*."

The Rat dropped the stick into the gutter and wiped his hand on his pantleg. "They've made us late on our rounds. Let's get going. *Mach schnell!*" The Rat threw back his shoulders, turned on his heel, and proceeded through the village. As he passed, he issued tight little nods to the shoppers who were slowly thawing back into the rhythm of the day.

Scarecrow stretched his loose lanky limbs upright, bent to give Odin's shoulder a quick pat, and then brushed his hands together. "*Auf Wiedersehen, Fräulein.*" His long legs quickly caught up to his patrol-mate.

Mari stayed still, clutching Odin in a desperate hug, until the soldiers were out of sight. She noticed Mrs. Nilssen making her way slowly toward them, holding a basket in one hand and leaning onto her cane with the other. Mari hopped up to help her across the cobbled street, but before she knew it she was engulfed in a hug. She felt Mrs. Nilssen's body shaking against her shoulder.

"Are you okay, Mrs. Nilssen?" Mari asked, surprised.

Mari felt trapped in a surprisingly strong grip as Mrs. Nilssen held her close and whispered in her ear, "I'm fine. Just give me a moment." After another long moment, Mari felt the hug loosen.

When she was finally released Mari was stunned to see the old woman grinning at her. "Let's go see Dagmar, shall we? Your Bestemor will want to know what happened here today, don't you agree?"

Mari picked up the stick and handed it to Odin, who chomped on it and fell into step beside the two of them heading home.

Mari was appalled at what she had said and done. She could feel her pulse racing in her chest and temples.

"Maybe we shouldn't tell Bestemor about this, Mrs. Nilssen. It will only upset her." She took the basket and offered her arm to Mrs. Nilssen for support up the hill.

"Oh, baby girl, she'll want to know about it all right, and I want to be there to see her face when she hears the story!"

Mari didn't have a hand free to rub Odin's ear, just when she felt she needed it the most.

Chapter Six

Clever Resistance

At her grandma's cottage table, Mari stared, open-mouthed, while Mrs. Nilssen related every detail of the encounter in the village. She paused repeatedly to wipe her eyes or catch her breath, not from crying but from laughter. Her version was peppered with giggles, grins, and nods from Bestemor.

The dramatic report Mrs. Nilssen shared was barely recognizable to Mari. Mrs. Nilssen told a highly embellished tale of watching a swaggering upstart of a German soldier being held at bay by a snarling fifty-pound dog, who then behaved perfectly at the mere whisper from a snip of a brave eleven-year-old girl.

"When the kraut-eater resorted to bullying and threats, your Mari looked him right in the eye and told him she had every right to be there. And then she showed how smart a Norsk elkhound really is. Especially one as rare and beautiful as Odin. I'm telling you, Dagmar, you can't keep calling Mari your baby girl. She showed no fear and left that goose-stepper no choice but to retreat in humiliation."

Bestemor pulled Mari close and kissed her on the top of the head. "I'm so proud of you, Mari. You *were* awake for the end of my story last night, weren't you? Oh, how I wish I could have been there to see you stand up to that terrible man!"

This was more than Mari could take. She pushed her chair back, eyes wide and mouth agape. She gripped the edge of the table until her fingers were white. "It wasn't like that at all! I WAS scared. I could have been shot! Odin could have been shot! It wasn't something to laugh at, not funny at all." As much as she loved making her grandma proud, these old women had no idea what had really happened to her.

Odin lifted his head from his favorite spot by the hearth and clicked across the stone floor. At the unexpected tone in her voice, he pawed at her leg. She sank back into the chair, but she couldn't seem to release her grip on the table to pet him, not even when he laid his head in her lap and whined softly.

Both women reached to pat Mari's hands, *tsk-tsk*-ing and shushing her, while Odin's tail *thump-thumped* their legs under the table.

Grandma scooted her chair closer to Mari's and wrapped an arm around her shoulder, tucking her granddaughter's head under her chin. "I know, sweetheart, you were terrified. That's what bullies do, they spread fear. But you didn't let them win! Don't you see that? Tonight at dinner tables all around the village your story will be told and will give people what they need the most—hope and laughter. You're a hero today."

Mari pulled away and looked up into her eyes. "I'm not a hero, Bestemor. I'm a target! The Rat hates me, hates Odin, and now if people are laughing at him he will hate us even more!"

Her grandma lifted Mari's chin, cupped her face in her hands, and shook her head. "We are all targets, Mari. The Nazis target anyone who resists, looking for excuses to display their power. That's why our own traitor Quisling and others like him joined the NS and decided to support Germany."

"That, and to get extra food rations and privileges," Mrs. Nilssen grumbled.

"A victory like you had today is one of self-respect for all of us loyal Norwegians in the village. It is a victory for truth. In the end, truth will win."

Mrs. Nilssen nodded. "Until that time comes, hope and love and laughter are the small victories we need to keep us going."

Mari was sorry that she had turned their laughter into such looks of concern. But at least now they seemed to understand how awful everything really was.

Grandma continued, "It's normal to be afraid. I am afraid of you being hurt. I'm afraid for Lise in Oslo, for the resistance fighters hiding deep in the mountains, and for your Uncle Otto—"

Mrs. Nilssen interrupted, "and I fear for my Olav and Lars, too."

Mari finally felt they agreed with her that this was not something to laugh about.

As if reading her mind, her grandma continued. "This occupation is awful. It is wrong and frightening. I wish your childhood was not being stolen from you with this hateful invasion of our homeland."

"But we can't stop fighting, even if it is only with our laughter." Mrs. Nilssen lifted her cane and tapped the floor. "Let me give you an example."

She smiled. "When I rode the train car to Bergen last week, an officer entered and walked right toward me. I rapped my cane hard on the floor," she demonstrated, "and asked, 'Aren't you Germans taught to tip your hat to an old woman?'"

Mari and Grandma both laughed, but Mrs. Nilssen lifted a finger to show there was more to her story.

"He stopped in the aisle, stood tall and tipped his hat. He actually looked quite rude and superior in the way he did it. But I just nodded and smiled and said, 'Thank you, much better.' Then, as he proceeded past me my cane *accidentally* slipped from my hand and tripped him!"

Mari joined in the hearty laughter this time. Mrs. Nilssen finally dabbed at her eyes and caught her breath long enough to say, "That's the fifth time that little trick has worked for me!"

Their laughter erupted again so loudly that Odin joined in, barking and racing around the table.

After Mrs. Nilssen left for home, Mari, Odin, and Bestemor walked the short path to the kitchen door for dinner.

"You were so strong and smart today, Mari. I thought you fell asleep the other night when I added an ending to the story, but you must have heard me. You told the truth, just like that little boy watching the Emperor in the parade."

Mari didn't remember an extra ending, but she did remember being able to sleep. "But what if The Rat is really looking for me, what if he tries to hurt Odin?"

"Come, let's help Sonja put the food on the table. If you start talking like that you'll have me worrying again!"

Chapter Seven

Nisse Cap Secrets

September, 1940

School ended early for the year not long after the German invasion on April ninth, but fall semester would finally begin tomorrow. Mari was looking forward to seeing more of her friends, even if she wouldn't have a new dress to add to last year's clothes.

"Hold still, little one, it's already late. And I'll need to iron this after I finish the alterations." Mama spoke past the pins pressed between her lips, working her way around the hem of another of Mari's dresses. "There's barely enough fabric left to make this wearable. You're growing taller every day, baby girl. When Lise comes home at Christmas you may be able to look her in the eye."

Every family photo showed how much Lise took after Mama and Bestemor: petite, round-faced, and blue-eyed with rose-petal skin. Mari longed to look like them. In-

44

stead she grew up hearing, "You look just like your Papa."

Her father and Bjorn were tall and square-shouldered, with oval faces, eager smiles, and large granite eyes—gray with flecks of amber and green. That, combined with high cheekbones and thick dark hair, made them undeniably handsome.

Handsome was not the look she'd have chosen for herself. At least she had their dimples, but she'd trade them for blonde hair and blue eyes.

That was the least of her concerns, though. The rationing and restrictions of the German occupation made everyday life so difficult. Papa was working such long hours on the trains, Bjorn slaved away at the bank, and Mama took in washing, ironing, and sewing for the soldiers. Even Bestemor spent hours bent over her needlework, making small souvenir pieces to sell to the Germans to send home. With the ration cards the Germans issued, everything cost more, and every *krone* they earned was needed for food and to save for black-market extras or emergencies.

Mari preferred to spend her time in her room reading or sitting with Bestemor and stitching, but she had many chores to do and errands to run. Odin, as patient as he was, could lie close and quiet for just so long before insisting that they take a run up the mountain or a walk through the village. Whenever possible, though, Mari stayed within sight of her home and yard, always keeping Odin by her side.

"Stand straight now," Mama insisted, tugging at the

loose fabric at Mari's waistline. "I'll settle for a few tucks in the band. That's all I have time for tonight. When I have more time, I'll redo the bodice with darts. I should have noticed sooner how thin you are becoming. If you get any thinner you'll disappear entirely!"

It was as if she had already disappeared. In the few weeks since Mr. Meier had been taken away she felt so much fear and anger, so powerless to do anything about the Germans and the changes in all their lives. Mari felt as jumpy as a rabbit these days, either freezing in place or darting at the slightest sound or motion. She flinched when Mama slid the dress down over her hips.

"Did I scratch you with the pins, little one?"

Mari mumbled, "No, Mama, I'm fine." She raised her arms and let Mama slide her nightgown down onto her shoulders.

Bedtime had become her refuge. The blackout curtains and flickering candles gave her home a snug, quiet glow. Papa and Bjorn complained about it, saying they'd be as blind as moles if the occupation continued much longer. Mari had even heard whispered stories of Gestapo night raids on some of the villagers, but there was no reason for them to come to her home. The Gestapo were the secret police, the worst of the Germans, the ones responsible for the orders to take away people like Mr. Meier.

She crawled under the covers and patted the bed for Odin to join her. Just as Mama leaned in to kiss Mari good night, Odin scooted his head up onto the pillow. They both laughed and kissed the two sides of his snout, then each other.

Mari clung to Odin and sunk into her pillow as Mama turned off the light and whispered, "Sweet dreams, little one."

~

Mari found Mama had fixed a special breakfast for the first day of school. There was no meat or porridge, but her eyes grew wide at the sight of a soft-boiled egg on her plate. Next to it was dark toast and a tiny dab of jelly.

"Thank you, Mama, but Papa should have this—we haven't had eggs or jelly all summer!" Mari slid her plate toward Papa, but he held up his hand and stopped her.

"It's a special day for you, Mari. You're starting back to school, and we count on you to do the best work you've ever done. This will be your last year in elementary school. You'll be studying with people you know and trust, friends you've known for a long time. But," he added, "you must still be very careful about what you say and when you say it."

Mari saw her mother's forehead crease and her head shake for Papa to be quiet.

"Sonja, we agreed, she needs to hear about this," Papa said, reaching for Mama's hand.

Mari felt a familiar twist in her gut, an uneasy feeling in the back of her throat.

Papa continued. "In just these few months since the invasion, the Germans have done all they can to make us

47

join their side. Too many are willing to sign up for the NS just to get more ration cards and hold on to their jobs. But for now, the teachers are still loyal Norwegians, at least the teachers here in Arne. You can trust Mr. Jensen. He helped organize the teachers to refuse to sign loyalty cards for the NS."

Papa shook his head sadly. "Who knows what it will be like for you in high school next year. But Mr. Jensen will be teaching you the truth."

Bjorn broke his scowling silence. "So far most of the high school teachers are refusing, too, but not all. You must be very careful what you say at school, even around those you've known all your life. Too many traitors have signed away their right to call themselves Norwegians! Those who join Quisling's Nazi-friendly party may as well hang out welcome signs to the Germans!"

Heads nodded around the table.

Mama covered her daughter's hand and spoke softly. "Little one, we need you to grow up fast, to lift up your eyes and see what is happening around you."

Mari had been watching, and she knew, of course, about those who had joined with the Germans. When she was in the village shops, she saw how their bags had more food, how their waistlines were not shrinking as fast as her family's. She overheard NS members defend their choice, saying it was "in name only," just a practical matter. She saw how others who heard such things gave them the cold shoulder, how everyone guarded their words around those villagers as carefully as if they were Germans. Since her outburst to defend Odin, she felt she was all eyes and ears, rarely speaking more than was necessary to complete her errands.

Mari pressed her back into her chair and scanned their faces. Papa, Mama, and Bjorn all wore the same look—worry. Bestemor was rocking slightly and caught her eye, winking and smiling. Mari wanted to run to her and bury herself in a hug, but the rest of her family expected her to "grow up." She stayed in her chair, but returned the wink.

Glancing down at the egg she expected her mouth to water, but the conversation had left her as dry as chalk. She picked up her fork and took a deep breath.

"That's more like it!" Bestemor proclaimed, reaching for Mari's plate. "You'll do just fine, and be the star of your class, my baby girl." She carried the plate to the stove, settling the egg into the still-hot water and resting the plate above the steam to warm the toast. "Mari is going to make us all proud. She's as smart as a whip and will figure out who can be trusted and who cannot."

She dug into her apron pocket and turned to the table, pulling on something tucked in there. With a flourish, out came a knitted red nisse cap. Bestemor smiled. "Mari, even if winter is months away, you'll want to have this on your head. Wait until you see how many of your classmates are wearing them. Even without a new dress, you'll be at the height of fashion!"

She set the cap on a chair and returned the warmed

food to the table. "Now, get busy with this elegant breakfast so you can get to school on time."

Mari giggled and her family laughed as Bestemor put the pointed elf-like cap on her own white hair and, with a hand on one hip, strutted back and forth in front of the stove.

Somehow the laughter calmed Mari. She chewed the egg slowly, holding the flavor in her mouth as long as possible. She ran her finger around the plate to gather the last of the yolk, but before she could lick it Odin was at her side.

"Yes, it is a special day for you, too," she said, offering him the last taste. "You'll take good care of Bestemor while I'm at school, *ja?*"

She rubbed his velvety inner ear and laughed at his twitching nose edging closer to the plate.

"Okay, enough, it's all gone, Odin! And no more time to waste." She carried her plate to the sink and hoisted her backpack onto her shoulder.

Bestemor was wrapping a shawl around her own shoulders. "I'll walk with you and Odin through the village. He can follow you up the hill to school, then he'll come back to me waiting at the edge of town."

"I thought I was expected to grow up. You haven't walked with me for two years. I'll be fine, Odin takes good care of me," Mari said, patting his solid shoulders.

Her grandma looked directly into Mari's eyes, then hugged Odin's head against her leg. "Yes, but this way he won't be passing through the village alone several times each day. Can it hurt for me to keep an eye on *him?*"

"Why . . . ? Oh!" Mari dropped to one knee and embraced Odin.

She felt as if The Rat was just outside their kitchen door, waiting to point his gun at Odin's head. She whispered in Odin's ear, "Stay close to Bestemor while I'm in school. Promise?"

Odin never missed a chance to lick a kiss on Mari's face.

She stuffed the red cap into a pocket on her backpack, stood, and gave Bestemor's arm a quick squeeze.

"Let's go, then, or I'll be late."

Chapter Eight

Lunchtime Lessons

"I wouldn't have believed it if I hadn't seen it myself. Mr. Jensen's pot-belly has all but disappeared—in only a few months!" Eva laughed, and then choked on the hard dry bread in her sandwich.

Mari and the rest of her class sat on the hill at the edge of the schoolyard, eating lunch in the shade of an ancient maple tree. She had been with these same friends and with their teacher, Mr. Jensen, since Year One. Until this year, she and her friend Sarah would often go off on their own, taking a short walk to find a quiet spot to eat lunch by themselves.

But Sarah hadn't returned to class for Year Six. When first-day attendance was taken, their class counted only eleven students. Five of their previous classmates' names were not called; they were nowhere to be seen.

"Mr. Jensen wasn't fat," Astrid defended their teacher. Her own father died when she was only six, and she sometimes slipped and called Mr. Jensen 'father.'

"Well, his cream-cake belly is gone. Did you see? His trousers are so loose now he's tightened his belt to hold them up," Eva teased.

Mari stared at the bread in her hands. Her sandwich was dry, too, and she knew she wouldn't be able to swallow even one bite. The talk at breakfast hung over her all morning.

She hadn't noticed Mr. Jensen's belt, but now she could feel Mama's hands pinning tucks into her own waistband. Everyone was shrinking in the waist. She looked from Eva to Astrid, then at Ingrid, Leif, Per, Greta and the others. Her classmates were growing taller, though. Most had grown at least an inch or two, as she had. In fact, Mari thought she was probably taller than Greta now. But all, even the boys, were leaner than last year.

She scanned the clusters of younger students. They too had grown, but none were as round and rosy-cheeked as they had been in the past. At least it seemed that way to Mari. Mama was right. She could learn much by looking up and noticing what was going on around her.

"Mari, Mari, did you hear me?" Greta asked, poking her in the arm.

"No, I guess not. What is it?" Mari turned back to the group and saw everyone looking at her.

"Have you heard from Sarah and her family?"

Mari's thoughts returned to how she had felt when she had stared at Sarah's empty desk as the teacher had called the first roll-call of the school year.

"No, I thought she'd be here. They must have decided to stay in the north a bit longer." Mari felt an aching hole in her chest as she allowed herself to admit how much she had missed her best friend, how much she had counted on seeing her today.

Leif shook his head and muttered, "You can't be that much of a baby, Mari. They're never coming back."

"Of course they are. And don't call me a baby. Sarah and her family went to stay at her aunt's in Nordland for the summer. They're just—they're probably needed there until after the harvest. Sarah will be back soon, you'll see." Mari glared at Leif, then looked around the circle of friends for support. Instead, she saw heads ducked or shaking.

Leif looked slightly apologetic, but still shook his head firmly.

Greta whispered in Mari's ear, "No, she won't be back. Mr. Jensen didn't even call her name. Sarah and her family are Jews, you know that."

Of course Mari knew that the Cohns were Jewish. They didn't attend church and their older children hadn't been confirmed. But what difference did that make?

Then it clicked. *They're Jews.*

Mari crumpled the dry brown bread in her hand.

Jews. Just like Mr. Meier.

Greta continued, "Papa said the Cohns were smart to leave so quickly. They probably made it north with some of their property and valuables, got away before the Germans took full control of our village. Once they saw what was happening, they might have made it over the border and escaped to Sweden."

Mari wrung her hands and blinked back tears. She might never see Sarah again.

Leif spoke more gently now. "It's a good thing for them, Mari. This way they're safe."

Astrid asked, "But what about the others who didn't come back this year? They aren't all Jewish."

Mari noticed that Astrid had finished her own sandwich but was picking at her cuticles until one was bleeding. She reached over and held Astrid's hands.

Per noticed, too, and patted Astrid's knee. "I don't think we'll be seeing any of them again, at least not until this mess is all over. Eugen and Risa each have older brothers who were being recruited by the Germans. If they signed up, those two would be here now and eating better than any of us, you can be sure."

Leif added, "Their families probably decided to get out of town, too. They knew that if their sons 'volunteered' for the German army, they'd be sent right away to some battlefront in Europe, while the Germans sit here safe in Norway eating our cream cakes!"

"But where did they all go?" Mari asked, surprised that she had spoken her thoughts aloud.

"Probably north. Or into the mountains nearby, if they wanted to join the resistance."

Per nodded. "As for Erik's and Jena's families, I didn't hear much. My guess is they went as far from the cities as they could. You know the German soldiers try to get the Norwegian girls to date them, offering chocolates, candies, and special privileges. Erik's and Jena's older sisters are very pretty," Per said, his cheeks and neck turning red.

Mari's throat tightened, and she struggled to catch her breath, feeling as if she were about to drown. Her own brother Bjorn, working at the bank. Lise, at school in Oslo. They had more to fear than she did, and she hadn't even thought about it. They were her strength, her sense of safety, yet they were the ones in the greatest danger.

"I HATE them!" Mari murmured, then brushed away a tear rolling down her cheek.

Mari felt Greta lean in and wipe her face with her kerchief. Greta asked her, using a gentler voice than usual, "Did you really yell at The Rat and tell him to mind his own business? I told my mother I doubted it was you. You barely say two words around us except about school work. But she insisted it was you she saw in the village yelling at the Germans."

"*Ja,*" Astrid whispered, "my aunt Gudren said the same."

Mari squirmed, wondering what she should say. If ever there were a time to disappear, this would be it.

But she felt Per's arm slip around her shoulder and heard him say, "Well, *I* believe it. Mari comes from a brave family of resistance fighters, right?"

"Shhh, you fool," Greta said, kicking his foot and scowling. "You never know who might be listening!"

Mari shrugged off Per's arm and turned to him, speaking through gritted teeth. "My family is just like everyone else, trying to survive. That's not resistance, it's common sense. I just told The Rat that Odin and I had the right to walk wherever we wanted to go."

Per chuckled. "That's no small thing, and quite a surprise coming from you. Your Papa and Bjorn must be coaching you now."

"What are you talking about, Per? They didn't even—"

Mr. Jensen rang the lunch bell and waved them back to class.

Mari gathered her things, tucking them into her backpack. Per waited and walked back with her. "I thought you knew, especially when I saw the Nisse cap in your bag."

Then he bolted ahead to enter the building with the other boys.

Chapter Nine

A Message in the Dark

"Get to sleep early tonight, ladies and gentlemen," Mr. Jensen said. "You were all a bit fuzzy-headed today. I can forgive that on our first day, but you must be at your best tomorrow. Every day, for that matter. You have much to learn and investigate this year. Dismissed."

The others shuffled supplies and chattered among themselves, but Mari packed quickly and hurried out the door. There, waiting next to the step, was Odin. As soon as she reached him he spun in circles, then leaped to lick her face.

"Silly boy, " she said, rubbing his neck. "It was a long day for you, wasn't it? For me, too."

Odin circled her several times then nudged the backs of her knees.

"Yes, yes, I'm coming." Mari started down the path toward the village, relaxed and smiling for the first time that day.

"Wait, Mari," Greta called.

Mari paused for Greta to catch up while Odin spun and barked.

"Sit, Odin. Give paw," Mari said, and Greta managed to pet his head and shake his paw at the same time. Greta's smile matched her own. Smiles always came easily when Odin was around.

"He's such a smart dog, Mari."

"Thank you." Mari patted Odin's shoulder and resumed her walk. She tried to read Greta's face as they fell into step together.

"This isn't the way you walk home, is it, Greta?"

"No. I've been helping Papa at the drugstore this summer. I'll go there after school to work a few hours every day. Unless we have too much homework." She looked at Mari. "You always walked home with Sarah, so I thought you might like some company."

Mari had been in her papa's store a few times on errands in recent weeks but couldn't remember seeing Greta there. "Do you work in the stockroom?"

"No . . . well, yes . . . sometimes. I just do whatever Papa needs at the time. Oh, there's your grandmother. Is she waiting to walk you home?"

Mari was happy to see her there, and to see Odin bound ahead to greet her, but something about the way Greta asked made her feel embarrassed.

"Bestemor just likes to take a walk into town for some exercise. You know, for her heart. She hasn't walked me to

59

school for years now."

Greta must have heard the irritation in her reply and patted Mari's shoulder. "I didn't mean anything, Mari. Leif shouldn't have called you a baby today. You may be the youngest in our class, and kind of quiet, but none of us are the same since the Germans came. Anyway, you're almost as tall as I am now." Greta hiked her backpack up and squared her shoulders, stretching as tall as possible. Mari laughed, doing the same. "I'm actually taller than you, I think. Let's let Bestemor check!"

They reached the corner where the streets divided. "Next time, Mari. Papa needs me at the store as soon as possible. I'll see you tomorrow." Greta waved and called, "Good day, Mrs. Swenson!" as she hurried away up the street.

Odin, Mari, and her grandma fell into step for the walk through town, their street gradually sloping downhill, dropping toward the fjord.

"Bestemor, have you seen Greta at the drugstore? I can't remember seeing her there. But she said she's been working all summer."

"Hmm, perhaps she helps in back with the orders. Is she good with numbers?"

"Oh, no. She's a wonderful writer, but always needs extra help with mathematics."

"Well, little one, it's nothing to worry about. Tell me about your day."

That name again—"little one." Before, it had always

made Mari feel safe and special.

Now, even though she knew it was said with love, she felt a twinge of irritation upon hearing it.

~

Mari had finished washing the dishes, all but Papa's and Bjorn's. Their plates of food were still in the warming oven, waiting for them to return from another long day at work. Mama was ironing at Bestemor's cottage, the little building just behind the main house, while Mari sat at her kitchen table doing homework, a surprising amount for the first day of school. Mr. Jensen had warned them last spring that this would be a year of serious study, especially after missing so many weeks of class last spring.

Odin stretched and yawned, then looked at her hopefully.

"No more playing for now, Odin. I'll be reading for hours from the looks of it," she said, patting the stack of books. "Settle in for a nap and I'll wake you when I need a break."

It was early September, a season when daylight still lasted long into evening.

When the light was fading Mari stood, stretched, and marked her place in the book. Odin was dancing at the kitchen door, eager for some attention and exercise. The yard was long and fairly narrow, level until just beyond Bestemor's cottage where it rose into a rocky wooded patch. Even in the low light, Odin managed to follow her throw and return his driftwood stick time after time.

Eventually she sat down on the garden bench, and Odin curled up at her feet.

Not long after that, as darkness settled in the yard, Mari heard the crunch of gravel on the path. She jumped up and ran to the gate. "Papa? Bjorn?"

"Shh, not so loud!" a deep voice whispered nearby.

Startled, Mari backed toward the kitchen door. There was something familiar about the voice, but she couldn't place it.

"Wait, don't go," she heard. "Give this to your father."

A small leather pouch was tossed over the gate and landed not far from her feet. "Be sure he gets it."

"Who are you?" she whispered, "What's your name?"

No one answered.

She edged closer to the gate, peering out into the dark, deserted road. She heard nothing, saw no one. Her eyes explored Mr. Meier's property next door, but she saw nothing moving, only deep, still shadows.

Odin nudged her hip, holding the small pouch in his mouth.

"Good boy, Odin," she said, as he dropped it in her hand.

Mari hurried right away to Bestemor's cottage at the back of the yard and burst into the room. Her mother was done ironing, it seemed, and was sitting with Bestemor, talking quietly.

"Mama, Mama, look at this. It's for Papa." She held the pouch in her open hand.

Mari saw Mama and Bestemor exchange startled looks, and Mama's face flushed.

Bestemor rose stiffly from her chair and took the pouch from Mari's hand. She tucked it into her apron pocket and headed to the window. "Look at the time, Sonja. I need to close the blackout curtains and dim the lights here. You take Mari home to do the same. When I finish, I'll walk over for a cup of tea."

Mama seemed as frozen as Mari sometimes felt, but Grandma gave her a bit of a nudge. "Sonja, get yourselves back to the house."

Mari asked, "But what about the package for Papa?"

Mama seemed to snap back to life and wrapped an arm around Mari, leading her toward the door. "First things first, little one. Let's take care of the windows and talk later, *ja*?"

Chapter Ten

Family Secrets

Mari objected, but Mama insisted she finish her homework as soon as the blackout curtains were in place. Mari had seen her startled expression when she had seen the little leather pouch. Why was she acting now as if nothing had happened?

When Mari heard footsteps in the yard she stood up, but immediately felt Mama's hand on her shoulder, sitting the girl firmly back onto her chair.

"Homework first," Mama said, then stepped out to the kitchen stoop before anyone entered. Mari heard their low murmurings. She thought about Per's comments that afternoon, slid off her chair, and tiptoed toward the kitchen door.

"Homework finished already, Mari?" Mama asked, leading Papa and Bjorn into the kitchen. Bestemor was with them, too.

Mari side-stepped to the sink. "Just one more chapter

of history to read. I needed to get a drink," She gathered her books and settled onto the rocker just around the corner from the table. Maybe they would forget she was there and say something that could explain what the pouch was all about.

By the time Papa and Bjorn had finished eating, Mari's reading was complete. She had focused so much on the kitchen conversation that even if she were offered a kilo of butter for a chapter summary, she couldn't tell one thing she had read.

Nothing had been said about the pouch, she was certain of that. She tucked the textbook into her backpack. Bestemor's nisse cap stuck out of the pack's side pocket where she stuffed it that morning. She retrieved it, folded it neatly, and slid it all the way under her books. She was surprised to see almost everyone wearing one that day, even the youngest. She tried to picture herself walking through the village wearing it, but the very thought of attracting the attention of soldiers caused her throat to tighten.

"Mari, come here, please."

Mama's voice startled her, and she stumbled as she rose from the chair. Odin stood and stretched, then clicked past her and settled himself under the table. Bestemor poured a cup of mint tea and set it at Mari's place. Papa patted her chair, signaling that she should join them. Other than mealtimes or chores, she was being sent away from gatherings at the table more often than not these days. She surveyed their faces, trying to discern if she had done something wrong.

"Sit, baby girl," Papa said. "Your lessons are not over yet."

Mari was surprised to feel a twinge of irritation when Papa called her that, thinking how seldom he even used her name. She could hear how much love was in his voice. Still, it just didn't sit right with her today.

"Remember our breakfast discussion?" he asked, looking intently into her eyes.

"Of course, Papa, but what about—"

"Wait, let me finish first, then questions."

Mari glanced at Mama, who rocked slightly, holding her half-filled cup with both hands. Bjorn leaned forward with his arms crossed on the edge of the table. Bestemor's hands tugged and turned a bit of thread with her crochet needle, automatically constructing something beautiful. All were looking at her as intently as Papa.

"This morning there was much we didn't tell you. We believed the less you knew, the safer you would be. But things are happening so fast, everywhere, you must know the truth." Papa's head slumped forward for just a moment, then he took a deep breath and continued.

"Bjorn and I are not working late each night. At least not at our regular jobs."

Mari remembered Per's words, and she started to reach for her tea. But her hand trembled and she pulled it back quickly, dropping it back into her lap to find Odin waiting there, his head on her knee. She ran her hand across his muzzle and began rubbing his ear.

"You must not tell anyone that we are working late. The Germans know our normal schedules, so it would raise suspicions."

"As if they could be more suspicious than they are now." Mari saw Bjorn's fists clench, his brow furrow. She barely recognized him without his perpetual smile.

"What are you do—"

"Just wait, listen."

Mari saw Mama and Papa exchange a look before he continued.

"We work with others to resist, to make things better for our countrymen and harder for the Germans. The less you know about how we do that, the safer you are." He reached into her lap and pulled her hands into his own.

Mari wanted desperately to feel safe, wanted to believe that Papa could protect her from anything, even the soldiers. She realized this wasn't true. Maybe it never had been, but she had believed it with all her heart.

She felt a familiar twisting, churning inside and was furious with herself for being such a baby. She fought back the tears that were filling her eyes and pulled a hand free and reached for her cup. After a few deep breaths and sips of tea, her stomach calmed just a bit.

Bjorn patted her shoulder. "Our little one is growing up." The warmth of his smile and firm hand helped settle her even more. Then she remembered the conversation at school lunch.

She clutched at his arm. "Bjorn, are they trying to make you join the NS, or even the army? Shouldn't you be hiding in the mountains?"

Bestemor shook her head and said, "You see. Even the children know of the dangers. With school in session, secrets will be harder to keep than before."

Bjorn managed a smile. "Don't worry. I have ways of making friends, of doing a few favors here and there. So far, I'm safe here."

Odin had come out from under the table and licked at Mari's face. Bjorn stopped to rub Odin's neck and continued. "I can do more good working at the bank than in the mountains, for now, at least. The day will come when I might need to leave, but not yet, little one. I'll know when it is time."

Mari pictured Sarah's family heading north as soon as the Germans came, and then remembered Mr. Meier bleeding and taken at gunpoint. How would Bjorn know, and how could he be sure to have enough time to escape?

She wrapped her arm around Odin and stroked his side. And what about Papa? What if the soldiers caught him doing whatever it is he does? Mari almost wished her family was with Sarah's in Sweden.

"That pouch arrived tonight by mistake. I expected it at another meeting place, but things do not always go as planned," Papa said, looking even more serious than before.

"What was in it, Papa? Why does it need to be secret?"

"You don't need to know. But this is not likely to be the last time that you find yourself in the middle of something you don't understand, so you need to be prepared."

Mari's mouth went dry. She couldn't imagine what might come next, but she tried to nod and look brave, as she looked around the table at the faces of those she loved most in the world.

Chapter Eleven

Call Me Mari

For the next hour Mari felt as if she were in a blizzard—confused, afraid, desperate for something familiar and safe. She learned that various packets or envelopes might show up from time to time, but she should take them directly to one of the adults, not look inside, not tell anyone. They might contain messages, even codes, or things of value to be traded for black-market goods. Bjorn's bank contacts and Papa's train travels allowed them to exchange things with members of the underground.

If someone spoke with her about things she didn't understand, she should listen very carefully and remember it exactly as it was said, but tell no one except Bjorn or Papa, and then only if they were alone. She should avoid saying anything about her family to others except simple comments about health or normal routines. She could never be sure if the person she spoke to was really checking up on her family.

Mari listened so intently she had barely moved other than to look back and forth at her father and brother as they emphasized various details. Her shoulders ached and her fingers were numb from clenching her hands in her lap.

Bjorn was especially concerned that she not overdo complaining about anything—not about the soldiers, the rationing, or anything that would bring her extra attention. "It's best to try to be invisible, to disappear into the crowd."

Mari finally interrupted. "*Everyone* complains! If I don't, I *will* look different from the others, especially at school. You should have heard them today! Per even said something . . ." she paused, suddenly realizing how dangerous that was ". . . about you helping the resistance." She saw Mama's startled expression, but Bjorn and Papa looked more angry than surprised.

Bjorn said, "Per has sometimes helped us, but he needs a stern reminder about keeping what he sees and hears to himself. I'll talk to his papa tomorrow."

"I'll do the same, but he's not the only one in your class who knows secrets. The safest approach is to say as little as possible. Or change the subject. Or just keep to yourself. Even if your friends are safe, someone else might hear what is being said."

Mari thought about the many times she and Sarah had stepped away from the others to walk or chat. How easy it would be if Sarah were still here. Mari thought about all the times she felt awkward in groups, how she mumbled, nodded, or said nothing when everyone around her was jabbering like gulls.

Then she remembered speaking up today, remembered that day in town when she spoke back to The Rat. She looked at Bestemor and remembered how proud she had made her grandma that day. Now, just when she was finding her voice, she would have to hide it again.

"What does Per do?' she asked. "Is there something I could do to help, too?" She amazed herself with that question, since the thought had not even entered her head. Staying quiet probably was the best choice—if she couldn't control what came out of her mouth when she spoke.

Mama said, "No, absolutely not, little one. Don't even think about it!"

Mama's head swiveled first to Papa, then to Bjorn, then back to Papa again. "Mari is to have no part in any of our doings, we agreed."

Bestemor's forehead creased, and she reached to pat her daughter's hand. "No, Sonja, at least not yet. We'll take things a day at a time, as we agreed."

It was Mari's head that was spinning as she realized what she had just heard. It sounded as if Mama and Bestemor were working for the resistance along with Papa and Bjorn. Papa's next words confirmed that.

"She's right, Sonja, we won't need her help yet. You know, though, that our safest messengers are the children and elders, and women like yourself who can pick up and deliver things at the military posts. The things you've seen and overheard have been critical in our planning."

Mari surprised herself yet again. "If everyone else is fighting the Germans, I can help, too. I'm not a baby any more, not your little one." She pushed back her chair and stood up.

"Mama, even you said how much I've grown. It's time for me to do something to help our family." As quickly as she had spoken, though, she felt her knees buckle under her. She sat down hard, feeling as limp and deflated as an old balloon. Odin circled the table and came to her side to rest his head in her lap. Not until she rubbed his ear was she able to resume breathing.

Mama's mouth was opening and closing like a beached cod, but she said nothing.

Bjorn tilted his head, looking at her first one way and then another. His eyes twinkled. "What has come over you? Are you really my baby sister? Or did the Allies kidnap Mari and leave you in her place?"

That broke the tension, and the comforting sound of laughter filled the kitchen. Bestemor dabbed at her eyes. "What did I tell you? Love and laughter will get us through the worst of times."

Papa cupped Mari's face in his hands. "You, my beautiful daughter, have grown more than just in inches. We will need your help, always."

"Tell me, Papa, what can I do?"

"For now, remember our warnings and guard our secrets. Speak your mind with us, when we are alone, but bite your tongue and duck your head when you are around others, especially if what they talk about isn't safe. "

Bjorn chuckled again. "That will seem normal to everyone who knows you in this village. I'm often asked why you're so shy, and I say it is only that you are young and easily frightened. But maybe you'll hear or see something useful because others forget you are there."

Bestemor added, "Tell us what you hear and see, but only when we are alone. Keep your eyes open for patterns, notice unusual activity. Even things like Mrs. Nilssen tripping a soldier on the train can give us clues about who is with us and who is not."

Finally Mama found her own voice again. "Most of us in the village do what we can in whatever way we can. The problem is not being certain who can be trusted. Even the small things send a message. It's only been a few months, but the Germans and NS members are already feeling the pain of our 'ice front.' Have you noticed the posters trying to make us speak German, to sit near them on the trains? We must keep making them feel as isolated as possible."

"I hate those posters," Mari said. "Everywhere you look they hang them, telling lies, pretending they are like Vikings. I wish I could tear them off the walls!"

"You've seen that they *are* torn down or painted over, haven't you? Let those who are out at night handle that for now. Have you seen *VH7* written around town on fences

74

and walls? For every poster they display, that 'Victory for King Haakon VII' sign shows up a hundred times."

"Enough for now," Mama said, pushing her chair back and stacking the cups. "You have school tomorrow and we must all wake early to work. Upstairs with you, baby girl. I'll be there soon."

"Mama," Mari said. "Could I ask you, all of you, one favor?" She saw each of them pause and wait with puzzled expressions.

"Please stop calling me 'little one' and 'baby girl.' Like you said, I need to grow up."

Bestemor and Bjorn smiled and nodded, but Mama rushed to Mari and hugged her.

"Mari, Mari, you'll always be my little one. You can't mean that."

Papa stood and walked over to wrap his arms around them both. Then, he gently turned them toward the steps.

"Mari, Mama and I will try our best to honor your request, but you must forgive us if we slip into old habits. You're our baby girl and always will be. Even if you should defeat the entire invasion army single-handed!"

Chapter Twelve

Bestemor in Danger

October, 1940

Mari looked up from her homework when she heard the kitchen door open. She rubbed her eyes, blood-shot from reading in low lights. Winter darkness was well on its way in October, and she found herself hanging the blackout curtains over the windows as soon as she arrived home from school each day.

She shrugged her shoulders to her ears, stretching first to one side, then the other. Mr. Jensen was true to his word about making the most of this last year together. School-work came easily to Mari, but both the work and the pace kept her focused and busy throughout the school day, then again for several hours each evening.

Bestemor stepped behind her and kissed the top of her head. Mari felt her grandma's fingers tuck loose strands of hair behind her ears. Then Bestemor rubbed her earlobes gently.

"You need a break, Mari. Take Odin into the yard for a turn outside. Then come back to my cottage. I have a pot of tea heating."

"I'm almost finished here. I'll need about fifteen minutes."

Mari was surprised when her grandma reached past her, closed her books, and said, "No, come now. And be quick with Odin."

Bestemor limped out the door and made her way along the path to the cottage. Mari wondered what was so important, but in recent weeks she had learned to listen for a certain tone of voice that meant "do as I say and save your questions," so she patted Odin's rump at her feet and did as she was told.

When Mari and Odin stepped through the cottage door, Odin circled and curled up immediately on the stone hearth. Mari filled the two empty cups on the table and moved the kettle off the burner. Her grandma was not in sight. She heard some shuffling from the bedroom.

"Have you propped your leg up, should I bring the tea in there?" Mari called.

"Leave the tea, Mari, come quickly."

She entered the room to see her grandma kneeling on the floor in the far corner, her back to the door. Mari rushed to her side, afraid she had fallen. Then she saw the open lid of the big linen trunk, with a stack of quilts and blankets on the floor next to it.

"Help me with this, hurry," Bestemor said, tugging at a grosgrain ribbon, the only thing remaining inside the chest.

Mari reached past her grandma to remove the ribbon, but found it was stuck in a crack between the base and the sides.

"Again, together this time. Pull when I say three. One, two, three . . ."

This time Mari anticipated resistance and used both hands. Bestemor gripped the ribbon with one hand and braced herself against the open edge of the chest with the other. On three, their combined effort lifted the ribbon and the wooden base of the large chest popped free with it. Mari caught her breath when she saw that the ribbon was attached to a false bottom, under which were a boxy radio and other equipment she didn't recognize.

"Hurry, Mari, put the radio over there. We've already missed some of the broadcast." Mari took it from her grandma's hands and set it on the bedside table. "I'll manage," Bestemor said, struggling to rise from her knees. "Plug it in, turn it on. It needs time to warm up before we'll be able to hear anything."

Mari followed directions, then checked to see if her grandma needed help. She saw her shuffling to the bedside and reached to steady her. She helped ease her onto the bed, then bent to lift her swollen leg.

"Not now, we're missing too much already. Pay attention, in case you need to do this without me." Mari watched her turn the volume knob low until there was only a soft hum like bees in a field of lupines. Bestemor laid her hand across the top, then uncoiled a wire from the back of the radio.

"Take this, twist it onto the nail in that beam, up in the corner, but not too tight." Mari squeezed past her and stretched to do as she was told. Then she saw Bestemor fiddle with the tuning knob. Slight squeals and whistles erupted, with snatches of static and voices in between. Finally a male voice with a British accent could be heard reporting news in Norwegian.

Mari tried to focus on what she was being told, but she kept seeing Mr. Meier with his hands tied behind his back, marched away at gunpoint, bleeding and helpless.

"Bestemor, you'll be killed if they catch you with a radio. Especially if you are listening to BBC."

"Hush, child, listen with me." She looked up at the wall clock. "We've missed most of it, but maybe there will be something to share."

Mari sat on the bed beside her and strained to hear every word of the broadcast, which wasn't easy with the reporter's odd accent and the low volume setting. In less than ten minutes, the radio was producing only static again.

Mari watched her grandma reset the dial to an approved Oslo station, then switch it off.

Before Mari could open her mouth to ask questions, she saw Bestemor signal for silence, then point to the antenna and plug. Mari retrieved them and watched carefully as she coiled the wires, tucked them into the back of the radio, and handed it to her.

"Now I'll show you how it is packed," her grandma whispered. Mari helped her up and offered her arm, leading her back to the chest.

"This is important. Put it back into the exact same space and tuck those towels around the sides. If this chest is lifted or moved, it shouldn't make any scraping sounds or shift around." Mari did as she was told, with a few extra nudges and tucks pointed out to her before Bestemor was satisfied.

"Now turn this just so," she said, pointing out a small mark on the false base, which needed to line up with a crack in the wooden side. "Press it down firmly, but not too hard. Evenly. Check to see if it feels solid all the way around."

Mari realized she had been holding her breath through this process and sighed deeply once the base was in place.

"We're not finished yet," she heard. "Sprinkle some cedar shavings back into the corners—not too much! Now the blankets and quilts." Mari lifted things in place and watched as Bestemor tugged a few corners here and there, making the stacks look well settled, not like things lightly laid out on store shelves. Finally she closed the lid, turned the key, and gestured for Mari to hand her the jewelry box. Inside she lifted a corner of the velvet lining and tucked the key under it.

At that point Mari began to breathe more normally.

But her grandmother was not quite done. Mari watched her reach for a lace doily, which she set onto the top of the trunk, even rumpling one edge a bit.

"Now, hand me my face powder," Bestemor said, catching Mari's eye and winking at her with a wry smile.

Mari watched as she removed the lid and patted the loose powder with the puff, shaking most of it back into the box. Except it didn't look like powder, and she didn't detect the familiar lavender scent she had expected.

"Watch what magic we can make with a bit of collected dust," her grandma said, holding the puff several feet above the chest and shaking it ever so slightly. Mari watched the dust motes float evenly down across the top of the chest, settling into the spaces of the lace as if it hadn't been open for a week or more.

Bestemor returned the puff to the box, closed the lid, and handed it to Mari with a huge grin. "Never too much of the dust, my dear! You don't want to ruin my reputation as a good housekeeper."

Mari felt an enormous sense of relief as she helped Bestemor back to the table where their tea had turned cold. Her grandma settled into a chair and said, "Heat the water again, Mari. Our work isn't finished yet."

Chapter Thirteen

On Her Own

For nearly an hour Mari sat with her grandma, repeating the various codes and phrases she would need to remember and use to share reports in town. Just the thought of the radio hidden in the bottom of that trunk made her chest tighten and her stomach twist. She knew her family was getting the BBC news from someone, but she would never have imagined Bestemor was the source.

Her brain approved of the logic of it. After all, Bestemor's cottage was set far back from the road, the bedroom wall tucked against the side of the mountain where no one could approach from behind the little house. And, as Bestemor said, "No one suspects a harmless old biddy."

But Mari's heart didn't even begin to agree—that her grandma was a biddy, or that any circumstances justified the risk of hiding a radio.

"Someone needs to take risks, Mari. And I am certainly not alone in this. There is little I can do at my age, and

I even need help with it, as you could see. Sonja is usually here 'ironing' for the 7:30 broadcast. But you did a fine job and will likely be called on to help again."

Mari couldn't deny her fear, but anger pushed at her heart as well. She stacked their cups and put them in the sink.

"I hate that Mama was called to cook and serve the Germans tonight! They call it a community meeting. But it's nothing more than a feast to stuff the bellies of those who joined the NS."

Her grandma cringed at the rattle of dishes. "Don't punish the china, I'd never get more."

Mari smiled and relaxed a tiny bit. She set the kettle back on to heat. Her grandma stood, leaning heavily on the sturdy table. Mari hurried to her side and took her elbow to help her to the bedroom.

"The Germans are very good at offering this kind of public reward for anyone who cooperates, you know that."

Mari nodded, nudging the chair out of the way.

"They love to make others," her grandma added, "like your Mama, cook and serve to see what they are missing. Then, like stray cats, they may even send the helpers home with a small dish of cream."

Mari pulled back the covers and helped Bestemor sit at the side of the bed. After she changed and was settled, Mari stopped her from pulling up the covers.

"Let me see your leg, Bestemor, you're hardly able to walk." She began unwrapping the strips of cotton gauze that covered the cut on her shin. "No more chopping for you, I'll get you all the kindling you need from now—"

Mari gasped as the last of the sticky strips dropped to the floor. She stared at the oozing gash in her leg. The two-inch cut was festering, the surrounding skin tight and red, stretched like sausage casing.

"I thought this was just a cut! You should have seen Doctor Olsen and had stitches! I'll go get him—"

"Hush, Mari, I'll tell you what needs to be done. Sonja already spoke to Dr. Olsen. He said to leave it open to drain, since medicines are so scarce. Fill the basin with hot water and hydrogen peroxide- he sent some for me to use. Get a clean towel from that drawer, soak it and wring it out well. Mari, are you listening?"

Mari looked up from the swollen leg and felt her grandma tug at her hand. She threw herself into a hug.

"Shh, I'll be fine, we'll all be fine." Mari felt her grandma's fingers rubbing her earlobe, then a kiss on her forehead. "We all need each other, more than ever before, but right now I need you, little one . . . Mari. Please."

Mari pulled herself to her feet, wishing she could go back to the days when she could really be "little one," when she always felt so safe. She brushed at her eyes with the back of her hand and swallowed hard.

"Start again, Bestemor. Tell me what needs to be done."

~

It was nearly ten o'clock by the time Mari had cleaned, soaked, and wrapped the leg. She was able to treat the open

84

wound with a poultice of comfrey leaves Mrs. Nilssen had provided. But the leg was still red, and hot to the touch. It needed to be treated with medicines. But the best medicines were only available to the Germans or NS members. Even aspirin would help with her fever, but there was none to be had.

Mari finally tucked the covers under her chin "I'll sleep on the sofa in case you need anything during the night."

"No, you won't. Home with you, and fast asleep, too. You have school tomorrow. Sonja will stop to see me when she finishes, which will be soon. "

"Isn't there something that will help with the pain?" Mari asked, tears threatening to spill.

Her grandma shook her head and sighed, then grinned. "Yes, there is. Bring me the bottle of vinegar—the white vinegar, not apple vinegar."

Mari hurried back with the half-empty bottle, feeling utterly confused. She handed it over and was appalled to see Bestemor sip at it, holding the vinegar in her mouth each time then swallowing slowly. After three small sips, she tightened the cap and handed it back.

"What . . . ? Why . . . ?" Mari stood holding the bottle and staring first at it and then at her grandma.

"Haven't you figured out by now that things are not always as they seem? Sniff the *vinegar*."

Mari untwisted the cap and knew immediately it wasn't vinegar, but couldn't place the slightly familiar, powerful scent.

"It's aquavit, silly. I trust it will be some time before the Germans decide we need to 'donate' vinegar to their cause! It's only for very special occasions, of course. To-night being able to sleep with this throbbing leg will feel very special. Now, kiss me, turn out the light, and get some sleep yourself," she said, settling back onto her pillow with a sigh.

~

Mari lay in her bed, rubbing Odin's ear. Sleep was not coming easily. Her mind kept replaying the radio scene, the instructions at the table, and Bestemor's leg. They had agreed that Mari would be walking to school on her own until the leg healed, delivering messages along the way in place of her grandma.

"Odin," Mari whispered, "you'll stay here and take good care of Bestemor until she can come with us again."

His paws shifted, and he rolled into her hug, huffing slightly before settling into the steady rhythm of sleep.

"I can't let you go through town on your own, and no one else will be here to take us. Mr. Jensen likes you, he might even let you stay with me in class for a day. But it could take weeks for that cut to heal." She turned her pillow over, poked at it, and settled herself for the umpteenth time.

"I wish you could do this for me. You probably already know more about the messages than I do—at least who to trust. You've been helping Bestemor make her stops and share her news all this time. And you didn't even tell me."

She smiled to herself, but the smile faded when she pictured doing the morning walk on her own. She actually already had learned, without realizing it, some of the stops and key words or phrases she had heard her grandma say as they had made their way together in the morning toward school in the last few weeks. She just had not realized what it was about.

Now she carried all the code words and names of villagers in her own head. Tomorrow, she'd be the one to use them on the way to school.

All by herself.

Chapter Fourteen

Messages Delivered

Odin definitely had a mind of his own the next morning. Every time Mari tried to step through the gate, he insisted on trying to leave with her. Papa and Bjorn were off to work already, and Mama was in the cottage fixing breakfast for Bestemor.

"*Nei*, Odin, sit, stay!" she commanded in a harsher voice than she had ever used with him, or with anyone, for that matter. Mari wanted Odin to obey, but wished with all her heart that she could give in and let him come along.

Odin sat, but his tail tucked, his ears laid back, and his head drooped. He looked so sad, she sank to her knees and hugged his neck, dodging kisses until she was laughing out loud and his tail was wagging.

But she had things she must do. Alone. "I'm sorry I yelled at you, Odin, but you *must* stay here. Guard the house. Bestemor needs you."

She rubbed his ears and kissed the top of his head before standing. She faced him directly and pointed at him with her index finger, just slightly, at which he immediately dropped to a sit at her feet and locked his gaze onto her hand. She held her hand upright, palm facing his nose, and barely whispered, "Sit, stay. Good dog."

She edged her feet backward, still holding her palm out and whispering, "Stay . . . good dog . . ." as she slid her other hand behind her to open the gate. But before she could step through Odin jumped up and squeezed past her legs through the gate. Then he turned in the path, sat and faced her, tail wagging, waiting attentively for the next command.

Mari sighed and shook her head. "Here, boy, come." She patted the side of her leg and hurried to the cottage at the back of the path. Odin romped ahead, happy to have won the battle. When she opened the door, Odin slipped in and found his familiar spot near the hearth and curled up, head on paws, but with his eyes still locked onto her.

Mama came from the cottage kitchen, drying her hands on a towel. "What's wrong? You should be half way to school by now."

Mari pointed toward Odin. "Odin really wants to go with me, will you keep him company when I leave?"

Mama stooped down beside him and rubbed his neck with one hand, sliding her other hand around his shoulder. She whispered into his ear and kissed his head, nodding at Mari to leave.

Odin's eyes had never left her. As Mari edged her way

to the door, he tried to jump up to join her, nearly toppling Mama who clasped her arms firmly around his neck, just long enough for Mari to slip out and latch the door behind her.

Mari covered the short distance downhill at a trot, pausing at the corner near the local fabric factory with the fjord to her back. She shivered, despite the run, and dropped her pack to the ground. Her fingers shook and fumbled as she tried to button her wool sweater.

Bestemor had explained that she could report to her contacts before or after school, but she raced down the road to the village in hopes of finishing in the morning. She had not slept well, trying to remember and rehearse how she would manage the messages. If she could complete her task on the way to school, it would be a great weight off her shoulders.

Many of the names shared with her last night were no surprise. She learned how particular code words that sounded familiar and normal really represented King Haakon, England, or Hitler. Certain comments or questions were meant to indicate progress or setbacks for the Allies. Once it was explained how the messages were passed, she recalled hearing bits of such innocent-sounding conversations when her grandmother walked with her on the daily trip to school.

Mr. Bruland, the postmaster, was the most unexpected contact. He didn't openly declare his membership in the NS, but Mari often saw him chatting with soldiers, even laughing and sharing jokes. He was clearly not honoring the "ice front," not trying to avoid or ignore the Germans or local sympathizers.

Her grandma had been quite clear, though, exactly what Mari was to say to him, and that he could be trusted.

She gave up on the last of her sweater buttons and slung her pack over her shoulder, forcing herself to get started. She reached the cobbler shop first, where she found Mr. Molstad sweeping the walk. Mari commented on how his clean windows reflected the bright sunrise. That meant: *Germans still succeeding on the eastern front.* Mrs. Nilssen was strolling past the shops and, after asking about Bestemor's leg, she admired the beautiful weather. Mari answered back that she had seen few birds out that morning. That meant: *no air bombardments reported last night.*

As she continued the climb through town, Mari passed Mr. Meier's jewelry shop, which had been reopened by another villager, Mr. Anderson, who was a proud member of the NS. It was no surprise when Bestemor warned Mari not to share any news with anybody if he was in earshot.

Short exchanges at the bakery and stationery stores took more time. She hurried along to school, hoping that Mr. Bruland would still be out sweeping his stoop when she passed. If she missed him, she'd need to stop in the post office after school and purchase a stamp. But there were often soldiers there in the afternoon, she knew, and she dreaded having to go back then.

Hoping did her no good, though. She turned the corner as the street rose toward the edge of town and saw that she was too late. When she peeked in the front window, she could see Mr. Bruland already behind his counter with a line of customers. So she would have to spend her day worrying.

She hitched her backpack higher on her shoulders and gripped her arms across her stomach, which suddenly felt a little upset. She gave the post office one final look and then broke into a trot to reach the schoolyard before the clanging of the bell.

~

On the way home, Mari's thoughts raced ahead into town, rehearsing her message to Mr. Bruland. But she forced her feet to match Greta's slow pace. While Greta complained about her test score, Mari nodded her head and mumbled uh-huh.

"You seem distracted, Mari. Are you worried about your grandma?"

"No. Well, yes, of course. I'm just feeling nervous about . . ." She let her voice trail off when she realized what she was about to say.

"Nervous about what? You can tell me," Greta said, taking her arm.

Bestemor had said to especially notice anyone who seemed to be pressing for information or eavesdropping. Maybe her nerves were getting the best of her, but Greta's question seemed suspicious.

"It's silly, I guess, but I'll be walking home alone for

the first time. I guess I really am a baby."

"I can be a few minutes late, Mari, if you want me to walk part way with you. I can go with you to the square and then cross over to go to work."

Greta sounded sincere, but Mari couldn't let her come along, not until she knew for sure that she could be trusted.

"Thanks, but I've got to grow up sooner or later. You won't tell anyone, will you? They tease me enough as it is." Mari shrugged Greta's hand off her arm and hurried on.

Greta said nothing more, and Mari wondered if she had offended her. But that was a worry she didn't dwell on. Instead her thoughts flitted to other afternoon walks home, with Odin and Bestemor at her side.

This was the part of day when soldiers were commonly encountered; they strolled up and down the streets of town, gazing in storefronts, nodding at passersby. They acted like they were just there to "break the ice" with people, to spend some money in the local economy and generally pretend like they belonged there. But Mari knew it was a ruse to keep an eye open for suspicious patterns of activity.

The two schoolgirls reached the corner in silence and separated. Mari rubbed a coin in her pocket, wishing Odin could be here with her for confidence. She tried to appear relaxed as she walked toward the post office, focusing on the cobbled walk at her feet and rubbing the *krone* until she thought she'd wear the date off.

She looked up from her thoughts to see Scarecrow and The Rat laughing and talking as they approached her on the sidewalk. Before they noticed her, she ducked into the bank lobby and hurried to the far side of a large desk. Mr. Olms was at the teller window.

She turned away to avoid his attention, but heard him ask, "Mari, are you here to see Bjorn?"

"*Nei, takk,* Mr. Olms. I—I had a pebble in my shoe and just stopped to get it out."

Dropping to one knee, she glanced up to see the two soldiers walking outside past the window. She prayed they wouldn't come in. She felt her neck and face burning with a mixture of fear and anger. She fussed much longer than necessary with her shoelace, then with her sock, trying to slow her breathing and calm her reaction. She still had a message to deliver. It wouldn't do to appear upset or anything other than routine.

Finally she stood and looked out the window again. They were gone. She waved to Mr. Olms and stepped out to the walk. Too soon she was standing at the entrance to the post office.

She checked her reflection in the glass, took out her coin, but her feet didn't move. She continued rubbing it, counting the people inside where she saw several of Mama's friends. The line wasn't long now. She reached for the doorknob, then jumped back and nearly fell off the stoop when the door swung wide open in front of her. Two soldiers stepped out.

Not Scarecrow and The Rat, but two others suddenly stood right there in her face.

Her *krone* dropped and rolled to the gutter.

"Careful, *Fräulein*, are you hurt?" one said.

Mari shook her head, stepped back a bit farther, and turned to retrieve her dropped coin. She kept her eyes down, glancing back at the shiny German boots waiting so close to her. The soldier who had spoken held the door open for her, but she shook her head again, as she crouched, pretending to have trouble picking up the coin..

"Come on, you'll be here all day if you wait for an answer," the other soldier said, starting down the street. He was quickly joined by his partner, their steel-heeled boots clanking on the cobbles as loudly as Mari's pulse was pounding in her ears.

Mrs. Finstad came out and walked to the curb. She retrieved the *krone* and handed it to Mari, chuckling. "They're gone now, Mari. Go and tend to your business. It's not so bad to be shy—they can't say you treat them any different than the rest of us. Now get your wits about you—you look like a cod on a hook."

She held the door for Mari, who managed to say "*Takk*" and forced her feet to carry her inside.

When it was her turn at the counter, Mr. Bruland smiled and asked, "What can we do for you today, Mari?"

Any semblance of calm she had gathered in the bank had disappeared on the steps with the soldiers. "One s-s-stamp, please," she managed to reply.

"Only one stamp is it? That's one thing we don't have to ration. Is there a particular kind you'd like?"

"Just a stamp for a letter to Hardanger, Mr. Bruland. Bestemor was expecting to hear from my Uncle Victor, but there's been no news. She wants to know if he is well." She placed the coin on the counter and swallowed hard.

The little bit about her "Uncle Victor" meant there was *no news about King Haakon VII in the last broadcast.*

"Here you are, Mari." He put the stamp in her hand. "Tell her I wish him well. She should send him my best wishes, too. Your uncle is a good man."

"I will. Thank you, sir." Mari slid the stamp into her pocket and turned to leave. She hopped off the stoop and walked briskly through the village, anxious to see Odin and to tell Bestemor that things had gone well.

Her mind was racing ahead so fast that she was startled when Mrs. Nilssen called to her from her porch. Mari hurried over, wondering if she had forgotten something in the morning message, or if she would be given information to take back home.

When she was closer she saw tears in her eyes. "Mari, run home as fast as you can. Odin was hurt today."

Mari's heart stopped beating.

Mrs. Nilssen's hands clutched at the porch rail and she continued, "I did what I could. Get home as fast as possible."

Mari stared at the woman, gulped for air, and said, "Odin? What happened?"

"Just go, get home and they'll explain. Hurry, child."

Chapter Fifteen

Kitchen Crisis

M ari burst through the door. She gulped for breaths of air between sobs and cried, "Odin! Where's Odin?"

Bestemor stepped out of the kitchen, arms wide, but Mari ducked away from her hug and squeezed past her into the kitchen.

"Where is he? Where's Odin?"

Her throat locked, and her feet stuck to the floor. Mama and Doctor Olsen were kneeling next to a blanket under the window. Mari could see them working on Odin, but he wasn't moving. He wasn't making any sounds. Bloody towels were piled on the floor.

Mari felt her grandma's hands on her shoulders, guiding her to a chair. That touch thawed her frozen feet. She shrugged loose and pushed past the table to the window. There she saw Odin stretched out on his side—his face bloody and his chest still.

"*Nei, nei, nei!*" she cried. She dropped to the floor and reached out, but felt the doctor block her arms and push her hands away.

"Be careful. You'll hurt him."

Odin's paws scrambled slightly, and she heard him whimper.

"Oh, Odin! I thought you were dead!" She swiped at her tears and leaned her head close to kiss his nose. That's when she saw what had caused the blood.

His right eye was swollen shut, and a jagged gash from his jaw to his ear had been shaved and stitched.

"He's sleeping, for now," Doctor Olsen said. "I can't be certain, without x-rays, but I believe his ribs are cracked, not broken. Breathing will be very painful for him, but he's lucky. If his lung had been punctured, I'd have to put him down."

Mari stared at Odin's battered face, at his chest barely rising and falling. He was alive, that's all that should matter. But something terrible had happened to him.

"What if it gets infected—"

"Just wait, Mari, until we finish here," Mama said. She held a towel wrapped tightly around Odin's chest, and Doctor Olsen taped it securely, strip after strip.

"How can he breathe?" Mari whispered.

"That's the idea, to limit his breathing so the ribs heal, but still allow him to breathe enough to avoid pneumonia. He'll need to be watched very closely in the next few weeks."

Mari felt like she would never take her eyes off of him again. She slumped against the wall, staring at her best friend, her broken friend. While Doctor Olsen collected his things and Mama cleared away the towels, Mari closed her eyes and let her tears fall freely.

She felt Odin stir slightly and saw Mama talking to the doctor at the door. Her fingers automatically rubbed the velvety lining of Odin's ear, and she felt him press his head into her hand.

"Odin, don't leave me," she whispered.

~

While Odin slept, Mama sat with Mari to explain his care. His jaw wasn't broken, but he would need to be hand-fed small soft bits of food for at least a week. He'd need help when he needed to get up and lie down. His wound needed to be cleaned at least twice a day. The injection he was given allowed him to be examined, cleaned, and stitched, and it would help him sleep through the night, but after that they had nothing more to help with the pain.

Mari wondered if Bestemor could spare a bit of her special "vinegar" for Odin.

Mari insisted that she should stay home with him, that she could get her assignments from school and complete them at home. Mama dismissed that as nonsense. She said Mari belonged in school, Bestemor belonged in bed, and Odin belonged right where he was, sleeping and healing. And it was Mama's job to make sure they were all where they belonged.

When Mari asked what happened, how Odin had been hurt, she saw Mama and her grandma exchange a long glance.

"We'll talk more about that when Papa and Bjorn get home," Mama said.

"*Nei!*" Mari snapped. Odin stirred slightly, and she gently stroked his paw until his breathing settled back into a steady rhythm. She whispered through gritted teeth, "Please, Mama, no waiting this time. Tell me who did this to Odin!"

Her mother sighed and slid down beside Mari, wrapping one arm around her shoulders. "It was the Germans, Mari. They did this."

Mari rolled into her mother's hug and sobbed.

~

Mari had fallen asleep. She woke to find Mama heating soup and Bestemor resting on the sofa. In minutes she heard familiar footsteps on the garden path.

Mari watched Odin's chest lift and fall. She scrutinized his stitched face, his puffy eye. She ached to stretch out next to him and fold him into her arms, wondered how long it would be until she could hug him again.

Mama noticed that Mari was awake and knelt beside her. "Sleep heals, Mari, and Odin is resting well. Come have some soup for now and we'll explain everything after that." Her mother rose and half-lifted Mari to her feet.

Mari checked anxiously as chairs were shifted and voices exchanged, but Odin only stirred slightly and continued sleeping while they ate. Mama helped Mari clear the table.

"Leave the dishes in the sink for now. It's time to explain." She wrapped her arm around Mari's shoulder and walked her into the living room.

"But—" Mari protested.

"Odin is fine where he is. He'll rest better if we leave him alone." Mama led her to the sofa where Bjorn and Bestemor were already seated.

It was time for Mari's questions, everyone seemed to be waiting, but she couldn't ask. Finally Bjorn began.

"I was at work at the bank when Mr. Molstad came running in, out of breath, and said Mrs. Nilssen needed me—immediately. I found her outside the flower shop trying to comfort Odin. She told me to get him home and she would send the doctor, then she would come and explain what had happened."

Mari leaned past Bjorn to look at Odin and felt tears fill her eyes. She chewed on her lip and swallowed hard to keep from being sick.

"We could see he was badly injured, so Mr. Molstad offered his cart. I was able to get Odin home, but he was having a hard time breathing."

Bestemor pulled out her handkerchief and wiped Mari's eyes, as she continued the report.

"The doctor got here soon after. Bjorn had to return to the bank. Elsa arrived while he was working on Odin and told me what happened in the village."

Mari saw her grandma's head droop, heard her take several breaths. When she looked up again she had tears in her eyes. "This is my fault, little one. After Sonja left to deliver laundry, I thought Odin was asking just to go out in the yard. I let him out, and he jumped the hedge and ran off toward the village. I couldn't go after him. It was close to dismissal time for the school, so I thought he'd meet you coming home. I thought he'd be fine."

Mari suddenly found her voice again. "Who did this to him? Someone tell me what happened!"

Her grandma wiped her own eyes and continued. "Elsa said she was sweeping her curb when she heard a disturbance down the street. When she arrived she saw a soldier aiming his gun at Odin and shouting. His partner pushed his arm down. She heard him say, 'Don't waste a bullet on that mutt,' and kicked Odin in the head."

Mari clutched her chest and struggled for breath.

"Odin must have stayed on his feet and lunged at him, because he kicked him again. By then Elsa was shouting at them to stop hurting the dog. They shouted back at her that the dog belonged to a pesky little girl, but Elsa said that we are cousins, that she would take the dog home."

Mari's face was streaming with tears and she could only catch her breath in hiccupping gulps.

"Elsa said that more and more people were watching by then. The Rat said to get him off the street. He said if he saw him running loose again, he'd shoot him. At least they left Odin there with Elsa."

"The Rat did this? I knew he hated Odin!" Mari's hands trembled with fury, and she gasped for breath.

Bestemor shook her head.

"Elsa said The Rat pulled his gun, but Scarecrow kicked him. None of that matters, little one, the damage is done."

Mama added, "And you heard Doctor Olsen, it could have been much worse. We'll take good care of him, Mari, he's safe with us now."

Now. But for how long? Mari walked around the corner to the kitchen and looked at Odin's swollen face, the shallow rise and fall of his wrapped chest. She pictured the oozing gash on Bestemor's leg and knew that there would be no medicines to treat him, that he would be in pain when he awoke.

Yes, he was safe for the moment. But things could still take a turn for the worse.

Chapter Sixteen

Recovery and Hope

November, 1940

Mari watched Dr. Olsen tap carefully on a bottle of yellowish powder, measuring a small amount into a paper packet.

"So, Mari, both of your patients are still improving."

She nodded. Through the first days, Odin's swollen face had stretched and reddened. He had been unable to eat even the softest bits of food. Bestemor shared her aquavit, using a little as an alcohol cleanser for his wound, but it was painful and didn't seem very effective.

During the first week Dr. Olsen had stopped by each day. He seemed pleased with Bestemor's progress. The poultice was helping Bestemor's leg, slowly, But when he examined Odin he shook his head and said, "We just have to wait and see. Don't give up hope."

Then one day he brought the powder. He wouldn't say

how he obtained it, and he provided very little. He showed Mari how to clean around the stitches, to clear away infected skin, and then apply the powder sparingly without getting it in Odin's eye.

After that Mari took over his care twice a day. She also cleaned and checked her grandma's leg, happy to see the redness diminish and the swelling subside.

The powder was making a difference. Odin's wound had almost stopped oozing, his skin was not as tight or red. Dr. Olsen portioned the powder in tiny amounts, so she stopped at his office several times a week to get more. She was desperately afraid that he'd stop giving it to her.

Papa said it was from the black market and must have cost the doctor dearly. It was meant for use with his human patients, and every bit he allowed Mari to use for Odin meant someone else would do without. When she remembered how Bestemor's leg had looked, how desperately she had wanted medicine to help her, she felt guilty.

She clenched her hands in her pockets and chewed the insides of her cheeks to keep from begging for more.

Dr. Olsen turned from his work and smiled with his eyes, since his lips were nearly hidden under a walrus-like mustache. "Wonderful! You've taken great care of them. I believe this will be the last you'll need."

"But his wound hasn't fully healed yet. It's still so raw." She bounced on her toes and wrung her hands together, trying hard to sound rational, not desperate.

Doctor Olsen folded the paper packet carefully and

placed it on the table. When she reached for it, she shook so much he took both of her hands in his.

"Mari, Odin has passed the crisis now. It will be a slow recovery. You still have to keep his wound clean and dry. But he will survive. You've been a fine nurse."

Mari drew in a sharp breath and stared into his eyes. "Are you certain?" She knew she should trust him, but she hadn't allowed herself to imagine that Odin would actually recover.

"Yes, little one, I'm sure." His gentle smile reassured her. "I'll stop by to see him again in a few days, to see how his ribs are healing."

Mari stared at the packet in her hands and felt her eyes fill. "I can never thank you enough for saving him." She tucked it into her coat pocket and kept her hand on it for safekeeping. "I know you should have kept the powder for other patients, but I'll find a way to repay you, I promise. It won't be right away, but I will repay you somehow."

He swung his arm over her shoulder and led her to the door. "You needn't worry about that. Tell your Mama I enjoyed the rabbit stew and thank her for me." He patted his stomach. "When Bjorn delivered it he offered to bring more, but I'm alone and you have a household of five. So any trapping he does should feed your family. He told you about the bones, didn't he?"

"*Ja*, and now I always do as you say. Mama cooks the bones to give a little flavor to the soup, then gives them to me. I split them and scrape out the marrow for Odin. He loves it!"

"Such a smart dog! It is very good for his healing ribs."

Mari could never erase the image of Odin struggling to swallow, unable to move his swollen tongue. On the second day the doctor found that two teeth had been knocked so loose he needed to remove them. The others were a bit loose, too, but the gums healed as his wound did, day by day. Mari had tried her best to get him to swallow, but it wasn't until she covered her finger with marrow and slid it into his mouth that she could feel his tongue begin to work again.

"He eats very well now, as long as it is soft and in bits."

"He still needs the marrow, as long has you can get it."

Mari nodded and reached for the doorknob. The doctor signaled for her to wait and stepped around the corner. He came back with a leather harness in his hands.

"Take this home, but don't use it yet. I'm giving it to you now so you can handle it often, let Odin see you with it, get your scent on it. When I come next, I'll check if he is ready to use it or not. He won't like it, I have no doubt."

Mari agreed. Odin had never worn a harness, not even a collar.

"Maybe he won't mind, compared to being wrapped up like a mummy." Mari wanted to believe that, but she couldn't imagine Odin tolerating it. She fingered the fine leather straps, the solid bindings. "It will take a while, but I will pay you for this, I promise."

The doctor chuckled. "I have no doubt you will, Mari,

but not with money, not in these times."

Mari tilted her head and examined his face for a clue about how she could repay him without money.

He reached to a high shelf and took down a ledger. "When I joined my grandfather, Bestefar Ole, here in his practice, this is one of the first things he showed me."

He opened the book to the first pages, and Mari saw dates as far back as 1896. She had a hard time reading it, since the script was very elaborate and the words were an old-fashioned version of Norwegian, but she could tell it was a record of office and home visits. In the far right column there were numbers showing payment for services. Some spaces were blank, and others showed entries like "2 chickens" or "roof repair."

Dr. Olsen continued, "You see, there is no hurry to pay, and the people here always find a way to make things right. Johan often has leftover scraps of shoe leather in his shop, so he was more than willing to make this for Odin. He'll adjust it if the size is not right."

Mari looked again at the leather harness, sniffed it and smelled the same pungent odor that met her whenever she pushed open the cobbler's door. She noticed now that the long solid straps had been constructed by stitching smaller pieces together with sturdy, even stitches. She couldn't imagine how much time it must have taken to complete it.

"I'm so grateful, and I'll pay Mr. Molstad back, too."

"No, that's not necessary. I told him this would clear

the slate from his son's birth last summer. I'm sure he'd appreciate a kind word about his craftsmanship, though. You can find ways to help others as time passes."

"I will, I know I will. I can never forget such kindness from both of you." Mari hugged his neck and headed home with one hand on the packet in her pocket and the other clutching Odin's new harness.

Chapter Seventeen

Greta's Secret

December, 1940

"Don't forget, your reports on the Crusades are due in a week," Mr. Jensen said. "Per, you turned in two late assignments so far this month. If this one is late, you'll stay after school to do your homework for the rest of the month."

Mari heard Greta snicker. She dropped her head to hide her own grin.

"Dismissed!"

Mari gathered her books and packed her bag with the others. When she entered the coatroom she saw Astrid staring out the window at the drizzling rain.

"This year Christmas will be miserable. Nothing about it feels right, especially this endless gray rain," she grumbled. "If only it would snow, or if the sun would shine for a few hours for even one day."

Mari understood how she felt. Since Odin and Beste-mor were recovering, though, she found herself smiling more easily and seeing a brighter future despite the weather and the Germans. She swung her arm around Astrid's shoulder and gave her a small squeeze.

"Things will improve soon. This can't last forever."

"*Takk*, Mari. I hope you are right."

In the schoolyard some classmates waited for younger siblings, others chatted, and a few hopped on bicycles to hurry off. On the bleak hillside their swarm of red wool caps offered a glimpse of hope through the damp fog.

Greta called out to Per as he sped past on his bike. "If you forget to work on that report you won't be rushing off every day!"

He laughed. "If you're so worried, do it for me!" and he pedaled down the hill in a spray of pebbles.

Mari and Greta had been walking to town together since the early days of the school year. Mari felt that Greta could be trusted, but until she knew for sure she stuck to safe subjects. After Odin and her grandma stopped meeting her, Mari sometimes took care of errands in the village on the way home. She had time for that because she nearly always had her daily radio reports completed on the way to school.

"What Per said is true, Greta. You write so well you could do the papers for all of us in the time it will take me to finish my own."

"*Takk*, Mari, but I'll be lucky to turn mine in on time.

111

Papa keeps me so busy after school that I sometimes have to get up early in the morning to finish homework."

A year ago Mari would have laughed at that, but instead she stepped a bit closer and spoke quietly. "What *is* it you do at the pharmacy every day?"

She watched Greta glance from side to side, then slow her pace slightly. When she spoke her voice was even softer than Mari's. "You shouldn't ask such things until you know there are no 'striped' students near. After more than six months, some still play both sides. They act like they are loyal Norwegians, then report what they hear to NS for a few extra ration slips."

Mari nodded and looked over her shoulder. In the earliest occupation days there were proclamations, some even from Norwegian leaders, making the Germans sound like friends, partners. By now it was clear that the German military control of the country was overwhelming, with hundreds of thousands of soldiers in strategic cities and everywhere in between. And as the news offered no hope of Hitler's defeat, too many Norwegians seemed to feel they would take the side of the stronger power.

Greta's red cap nearly touched Mari's. "The less you know about details, the better for all of us. I work with Papa and his friends—" she looked around quickly, then continued in a quiet voice, "to circulate the *Jossing* papers."

Mari grabbed Greta's hand and squeezed. "Really?" Mari whispered. She scoured her friend's face for any sign of teasing and instead saw Greta's wide eyes, nervous smile, and nodding head.

"Really," Greta replied, squeezing back. "Wearing red caps and paper clips on our collars is not enough. We may not be able to fight them with weapons . . . yet . . . but we can drive them crazy with our humor and strength. That's what makes the *Jossing* papers so powerful."

Greta's voice increased a little in volume with excitement, but Mari touched her own lips to quiet her. They were nearing the edge of the village, so Mari tugged her hand and led her off the path to the edge of the woods.

"Greta, whatever you're doing is dangerous! How can your own father let you take a risk like that?" Mari pictured her family sharing bits and pieces of how they were part of the quiet resistance, always keeping her at arm's length from the details. How could Greta's family put her in such danger?

"Living in Norway is dangerous for all of us now. I insisted on doing what I can. Others are doing much more than I do."

Mari's confusion must have been apparent, because Greta continued, "Those ridiculous German posters don't tear themselves off the walls overnight, you know."

"Greta, you aren't out after curfew? What if you get caught?"

"No, I'm not. But some in our class are." She stared knowingly into Mari's eyes. "Some who have trouble getting homework turned in on time. The jokes in the paper about Bergen's street urchins making trouble for the

Germans aren't far from the truth here in Arna."

Mari's recent optimism was overwhelmed by fear: for Greta, for Per . . . for Bjorn? The knot in her stomach nearly bent her double.

"Oh, Greta, it's not worth it! It won't make the German's leave! There are so many of them. And you could all end up in a prisoner camp, or worse!' She fought back the tears that filled her eyes, but one ran down her cheek. She let go of Greta's hand and wiped her face.

"You can't mean that." Greta's voice wasn't loud this time. It was deep, slow, steady. She sounded strong, almost like an adult. "This is OUR country, not theirs. They have taken our land, our ships, our homes, even our food."

Mari gulped back her tears and took a long slow breath. She was astonished by the look in Greta's eyes. Something about it reminded her of Odin.

"We can't let them take everything—not our pride, our hope. If we mock them and deny their power, they can't really win." Greta's voice had softened, and Mari saw tears filling her eyes, too.

She reached for Greta's hands again and held them, "I'm proud of you—"

"What's the matter, are you hurt?" Leif called to them from the path and headed in their direction. The girls exchanged quick looks and gathered their things.

"Just some girl talk, Leif. Nothing you'd care to hear about," Mari said. Hand in hand, the two girls headed back to the path. But Leif held his ground.

"Oh, sorting out broken hearts?" he teased.

Greta made her way past him, pulling Mari along. "Perhaps. But you can follow us all day and never hear *your* name mentioned."

The girls laughed and looked over their shoulders at him.

He grinned and waved, turning toward home.

Chapter Eighteen

Company for Christmas

Mari lifted her face to the snow and stuck out her tongue. Then, slightly self-conscious, she grinned at her childishness and glanced around to see if anyone had noticed. The snow and cold arrived just as she was starting winter break from school. She adjusted the heavy backpack on her shoulder and stuck her tongue out once more.

"Mari, can you spare a few minutes?" Mrs. Nilssen called from her porch.

"Of course," Mari replied.

When she crossed the street, she saw that the porch was already cleared of snow but the steep stone steps were not. Mrs. Nilssen signaled her to come inside.

"I'll be happy to clear the steps and path for you," Mari said, leaving her boots on the mat by the door. "Where is the broom?"

"In a moment, child. First I have news for you to take

home. Then I'll be very grateful for your help." She leaned on her cane and rubbed her left knee. "This cold and snow arrived just in time for the holidays, but it's always too soon for my aching joints."

Mari had heard her grandma say the same for the past two mornings. There was only a dusting of snow on the way to school that morning, but it was now several inches deep.

"Sit down, child, I have a message for you to take home." She patted the sofa cushion and Mari joined her, suddenly nervous. She stared at the toes of her woolen socks, hoping the news was good but expecting the worst.

"There are new posters and fliers all over the village today, and the same is true all across Norway, so they say. Hitler has ordered that all Norwegians must 'invite' a German soldier to their homes for a traditional holiday meal and celebration! Can you imagine such a thing?"

Mari felt as if she had been slapped in the face. And that is exactly what this was—a slap in the face at every loyal Norwegian. Already flags, traditional clothing, and patriotic songs were expressly forbidden. Mari's mind flashed to past Christmases at home and in the village. *Jul* traditions included all of those things, and now German soldiers would come into every home to enforce the ridiculous ban?

Rationing was so tight that potatoes were the only reliable food, sugar was impossible to find, and flour was more chalk than wheat, causing impressive farts from anyone who ate it. Now, this dreadful proclamation meant the villagers would have to share their meager fare with soldiers and tolerate them in their homes at Christmas time.

Mari saw her thoughts reflected in Mrs. Nilssen's face. "It feels like more than we can take, I know. Like everything else, we have no choice in the matter. A list of names will be posted tomorrow, matching families with soldiers. I thought Sonja and Dagmar would want to know right away."

"Yes, of course," Mari muttered, still stunned at the news. "I'll sweep for you and then head right home to tell them."

~

Mari lay in her bed, rubbing Odin's ear and trying not to hug his still-tender ribs too hard. She stroked the stubbly fur on his jaw and kissed him on the forehead.

"I don't care what they say, I won't be in the same house with one of them." Odin stretched back and licked her salty face.

"And I won't let you be here either, Odin. How can they expect us to sit in the same room, to act as if nothing ever happened to you? Mama said I could stay silent, she would say I have a sore throat. But I won't do it. I just won't. They can't make me."

She wiped her face and rocked him in her arms.

"Mari? Are you awake?"

At the sound of her brother's voice at her door, she pulled the covers over her head.

"I see you there, little turtle. Hiding. But you may as well come out and face facts." He perched on the foot of her bed and patted her leg.

Mari stayed still, but Odin tossed the covers back and pulled free of her hug. He gave her face a few more licks before nesting the covers and settling himself against Bjorn's leg.

"Now it's your turn, Mari. Odin is willing to listen, so you should, too."

At the sound of his name, Odin's tail thumped the bed, making her smile in spite of herself.

"That's more like it. We can't see the good in a bad situation with our eyes closed, you know." Mari humphed at him and tugged at the covers, but she couldn't budge them against the pressure of Odin's and Bjorn's weight.

"Oh, you win," she grumbled. "But that doesn't mean I'll change my mind."

Bjorn laughed and said, "Then don't join us. You'll be sorry, though. The only way we'll have our traditional holiday pork is if we invite the swine to our tables!"

Mari laughed and then kicked at him. "It's not funny, and you know it."

"But it is, in a way," Bjorn continued. "You'd be surprised at how many jokes are flying about this situation. They'll end up in the *Jossing* papers, too. We'll be laughing straight through to the New Year, I have no doubt. It's becoming a competition to have something printed."

When Mari told her family about Greta's activities,

they admitted they were aware of her involvement. Papa's job on the trains and Bjorn's work at the bank put them in position to overhear and report actual news, not just the propaganda that appeared in the censored local papers. They also contributed overheard jokes and helped to distribute papers.

Mari sat up and petted Odin. "You think you'll be laughing when a soldier is sitting at OUR table, eating Mama's cooking?" She stared accusingly at Bjorn. His eyes dropped to the floor for a moment, and she saw him swallow hard. Maybe she could win him over, and they could convince the rest of the family to refuse.

He looked up and replied with a surprisingly cheerful tone. "We *should* be laughing at them. If they were in their barracks they'd be eating much better and having a good time with their fellows. Here they'll eat the scraps we offer, face the 'ice front,' and go home with a belly full of gas!"

His hand covered Mari's, then slid down to rub Odin's side. "You know how much they hate being treated like the pigs they are, on the streets, the trains, everywhere. Since they posted their 'Declaration' that anyone who refuses to sit next to a soldier on the trains will be arrested, we all crowd into the standing space at the end of the train cars and leave empty seats with soldiers."

Mari nodded, smiling at the cartoon of that scene she had seen in the *Jossing* papers not long after the declaration appeared. It reminded her of the faces of soldiers trying to speak Norwegian. Most people in town acted as if they couldn't understand German, leaving the soldiers to struggle and sputter in Norsk.

She felt a warmth rise in her face as anger gripped her chest. She pictured one of them at her table at Christmas. "The ice front does nothing to stop them! They think we are ignorant peasants and laugh at us behind our backs!"

"It does more than you realize, Mari. So do the jokes, and sharing radio reports and news in our secret papers. Why else would they make such stupid declarations and try so hard to put a stop to it?"

He reached for her hand again and held on to it this time. "We need to remember who we are, to stand together, to see them as the enemy. It really is working. In the last few months there are fewer people joining the NS, fewer of our countrymen willing to abandon everything they believe in for a better job or a bit of cream cake. No one wants to be treated as if they are invisible."

Mari pulled her hand from his and scrunched down under the covers. "Maybe you're right, but I haven't changed my mind. I won't be in this house with a soldier."

Odin slowly rose and moved to her side, slumping into her arms with a heavy sigh. Bjorn stood and bent to kiss the top of Mari's head.

"We'll see. It's not until next week. And Lise will be home from Oslo tomorrow. Maybe she can help you see what must be done. Sleep well, little one."

Chapter Nineteen

Lise Arrives

Odin stopped digging and snuffling the snow-covered leaves and peeked out at her through the pine branches when Mari called. She knelt in the powdery snow and patted her leg, keeping the harness hidden behind her back. Odin gave the woody debris one last sniff and trotted to her side.

"Good boy, my good boy," she said, circling his neck with one arm. "Sit. Stay." She slipped the leather strap over his shoulders and reached under his chest for the bindings.

Learning to accept the harness and leash had challenged them both. His loyalty and obedience were strained to their limits for days on end as she urged him to cooperate, to stop scratching and chewing at the leather. She marveled at his rare display of elkhound stubbornness and considered it a victory when he walked on a leash at her side while they paced their long yard. The look on his face and his drooping tail made his opinion about the harness perfectly clear.

Many more days of practice were necessary before they could walk together down the path to the village. She never removed the harness until they were well away from town and safely back inside the gate or high up on the mountainside. Odin relished his romps through the treeline and returned when called, grudgingly accepting the harness for the walk home.

Mari fastened the last of the bindings across his chest, then kissed his head. "What a good boy you are. Lise will be home with Papa tonight. We've got to start the soup and do some decorating. It's nearly dark."

Gathering up an armful of pine boughs she stood at his side. "Ready? Heel."

They made their way down the mountain trail side by side, without so much as a tug on the leash.

~

"Are you sure you don't want more soup?" Mama asked yet again. "You are so thin, and we have real meat in this batch, thanks to Bjorn."

"*Nei, takk,* Mama. I made a sandwich and ate on the train," Lise answered. "I should help you and Mari clear things up." She pushed back her chair, then laughed as Bestemor and Papa each tugged at a hand to lead her to the sofa.

Mari wanted to abandon the sink and sit with them, but at least they no longer sent her to bed when important things were discussed. She washed as quietly as possible so she wouldn't miss a word.

"Go on," Bjorn urged. "What else is happening at University?"

Last year at this time, Lise had regaled them with reports of hospital experiences, study projects, and various pranks her friends had played against each other. Her program in nursing was more than half complete last year, her work at the hospital and in classes involved more and more responsibility. But none of that was the topic of interest this year.

"Oslo is a miserable place to be, truly, with the traitor Quisling dancing like a puppet on the Nazi strings." Lise paused for a sip of tea. "It's bad enough that the German forces are all over the country, using our North Sea harbors here in the west, blocking the Arctic passages in the north. Since they announced the end of the monarchy and took over the congress in September, they've turned our capital into a 'Little Berlin.' They make the laws, run the courts, and call our country 'New Norway.' It's disgusting."

With the last of the dishes on the shelf, Mari hung the towel to dry and hurried to join them. She curled up on the floor at Bestemor's feet, hanging on every word. Mari noticed Odin ease himself up from his mat near the stove and clicked to Lise's side, resting his head on her knee. She smiled when she saw her sister's fingers explore his healing scar, then reach for Odin's ear, rubbing gently. Mari had grown up sitting across from her sister, hearing her laugh and tell stories at meals and in this room. Having Lise home made it feel at least a bit like the holiday season, despite the topic of conversation.

She was startled from that rare feeling of tranquility when Bjorn slammed one fist into the palm of his other hand, his voice quiet but fierce. "Oslo is OUR capital, not the Germans'. With all the University students, so many citizens there, why doesn't anyone make an effort to stop this?"

The anger in his voice was unmistakable, but Mari picked up a sense of desperate pleading as well.

Lise smiled calmly at Bjorn. "Oh, there is a very active secret resistance, of course. We get news of ways they interfere with what's going on. They find and share military secrets, collaborate with Allied spies. That does help lift our spirits. But Hitler has stationed thousands of soldiers in and around the city. There's not that much the resistance can do."

Bjorn shoved himself to his feet, crossed the room, then paced back and forth between the kitchen and living room. "At least something is being done. We do what we can here, but the University group is leading the way. I'd like to be there to help almost as much as in the mountains with our fighters. Instead I'm stuck at the bank, forced to grin and jabber with the invaders, to gather jokes and bits of overheard conversation. I never even learn if it has proved useful."

Papa leaned back in his chair. "Bjorn, the same is true for me at the station. But we each must do what we can.

It's all the little things we do that torment them and keep them on edge. All the time and energy they spend trying to stop such annoying things is a drain on their effort to run Norway—and the rest of the world."

"They want to do more than run things, Papa." Mari noticed a change in Lise's voice, saw her forehead crease before her sister propped her elbow on her knee and covered her face with one hand.

"What is it, child?" Bestemor leaned across the coffee table and patted her sister's arm.

"Lise, has something happened?" Mama asked.

Mari was startled to see her sister look up with tears in her eyes. She didn't remember ever seeing Lise cry, and her stomach tightened. The room was so silent Mari could hear Odin's soft wheezes.

"Tell us." Papa swung his arm around Lise's shoulder, his voice no more than a whisper.

Lise sat up, wiped at her eyes, and forced a smile. She looked directly at Mari, holding her gaze for a moment before she began.

"Girls my age, and some even younger, are the target of unwanted attention from the soldiers."

Mari remembered the lunchtime conversation from a few months ago, on her first day back at school, when Per had told them how German soldiers had been trying to get Norwegian girls to date them, offering sweets and special privileges.

Lise swallowed hard and continued. "At first some

even found it exciting, to be wined and dined by the soldiers, to get extra gifts, to be with someone in power. At the hospital and on campus there are many officers with grand manners and medals on their chests who act as if we should swoon at their feet."

Lise caught Mari's eye, then looked away before continuing.

"We learned that it is official Nazi policy for the soldiers to work their way into our lives, even to marry local girls. They feel it will 'ensure the future of our united superior countries.' She rested her head on her hand again.

Mari's racing heartbeat pounded in her ears. The silence in the room seemed to scream at her.

She suddenly recognized something different. Lise wore a ring Mari had never seen before. A thought as bitter as poison flooded her mind. Mari struggled to her feet and bolted from the room and out the front door.

She was barely past the step when she dropped to her knees, heaving and spewing Mama's soup onto the cobbled path.

She heard the door click shut and felt a hand on her shoulder, then a hug. Instead of Mama's or her grandma's voice, though, it was Lise.

"I shouldn't have talked about that with you there, Mari, I'm so sorry. You've grown so much while I was away, I don't see you as a child anymore."

Mari tried to spit out the taste of bile, then leaned into her sister's arms, ready to cry.

"What about Erik? How can you marry a soldier? How can he let you?" Mari asked, pushing back from the hug and staring into her sister's eyes.

Chapter Twenty

Unexpected News

Mari and Lise returned to the family a few minutes later, arm in arm.

"What—what in the heaven's name happened out there?" Papa sputtered. "You two look as smug as hens on the nest. Are you all right now, little one?"

The two sisters exchanged knowing glances before Lise replied. "Mari was just a bit confused. I'd better share my news with all of you, too, before you jump to the wrong conclusions."

Mari wanted to head to the kitchen to make herself a fresh cup of mint tea, but first she leaned back against the wall, pleased to be the first to hear the truth about the ring. She was delighted to watch the expressions on the faces around the room while Lise explained.

Lise extended her hand over the coffee table and wiggled her fingers. "Erik and I are engaged! Even Germans don't pursue women with a ring—at least for now."

Everyone jumped up and spoke at once, laughing and congratulating her. Mama and Bestemor wrapped her in hugs while Papa kissed her cheek and Bjorn admired the ring. Mari refilled the teakettle and set it on the stove. When the excitement subsided enough for everyone to settle, she filled fresh cups and joined them.

"Why didn't you tell us sooner?" Mama said with just the hint of a pout. "You and Erik said your wedding plans would wait until after the Germans were defeated. When did you change your minds?"

Lise reached to hold her mother's hand. "I'm sorry, but I couldn't say anything in my letters. They've been reading some of the students' mail, especially those of us who are suspected of organized resistance."

Mari noticed Bjorn and Papa nodding while Lise continued. "I claimed to be engaged for more than a year when the soldiers were too persistent, but without a ring they doubted my story. I tried to tell them I didn't wear a ring because of working at the hospital. But when Erik went home to help with harvest, he returned with his grandmother's ring. Now I wear it everywhere, and it has been a great help."

Bjorn tugged at Mari's braid. "And little one here was the first to notice it! I thought, Mari, you were disappointed when the invasion made them delay their plans to marry. Why were you so upset to see that Lise's engaged?"

Mari felt her face flush and she ducked her head. Her mistake seemed so childish now.

Lise answered for her. "She noticed the ring while I was telling you about the soldiers. She thought I was engaged to a German."

Mari expected laughter. Instead she saw Mama and Bestemor clutch at Lise's hands. She saw Papa's forehead crease and Bjorn's hands clench his cup as he shook his head.

Lise looked around at all of them. "I'm sorry to say that is true for some of my classmates. But you all know I would never, *ever,* allow such a thing to happen to me."

Mari reached across the table to squeeze her sister's hand. "Well, I wish Mama and Papa would say they will never, *ever,* allow a German to sit at our *Jul* table."

She saw the puzzled look on her sister's face, and Mama's defeated expression. Before she had to listen again to all the reasons why they had no choice, Mari pushed away from the wall and strode toward the stairs.

Papa reached out and wrapped his arm around her waist, pulling her to his side. "Mari, no more running and hiding. Stay here and help us explain to Lise. We couldn't write to her about Odin, so she should hear from you how badly hurt he was. And why you feel so strongly about the Christmas visit."

"The declaration about *Jul* 'invitations' applies across the country," Lise said. "Mama and Papa can't refuse or they would be arrested. You don't want that, do you?"

"Of course not," Mari nearly shouted, "but I won't be here! Odin and I will hide on the mountainside or in Mr.

Meier's empty shed, but I won't be in this house with one of them!" Tears streamed down her face and she felt Odin press against the side of her leg.

Papa sat on the sofa and pulled her onto his lap. She buried her head on his shoulder, only half-listening as the others discussed their feelings about the visit and how they would handle it. Her hand dropped to Odin's neck, and she buried her fingers in the scruff of his neck.

~

"Wake up, baby girl. We've got a busy day waiting." Mari pushed back the covers and saw Lise holding out her clothes. "Tomorrow is Christmas Eve and Mama's list for us could take three days to finish. I'll be downstairs."

Mari hurried to dress and wash up, trying to remember how she had ended up in bed. She was too old and grown for Papa to carry up the stairs. Maybe.

At the table Lise went over their list of cleaning, polishing, and decorating. "Finish your tea, and don't crack a tooth on the tiles," she joked, pointing to the hard dark toast. "You slept through most of our planning last night, so I'll fill you in while we work."

Bjorn had learned that each "guest" would be given full details about the family members of the household. Their orders were to explore the house and account for everyone, keeping an eye out for flags, resistance newspapers, and anything in support of 'old Norway'. That's why Mama and Papa had insisted Mari should join them at the table.

Mari was stunned to hear that they had found a compromise she could accept. During the soldier's time in the house, Mari and Odin would stay in Bestemor's cottage.

They would say she had flu, so Bestemor was sleeping in the house and Mari was staying in the cottage. They'd tell the soldier they did that to keep him from carrying infection back to the other soldiers at the barracks. Odin could stay there with her, too.

Relief was the richest gift she could have hoped for this year. She found herself able to clean and decorate with a much lighter heart, although resentment still hovered at the edges of everything she did. Lise reminded her several times that the German soldier's visit would only last a few hours. When it was over the family could enjoy the rest of the holiday together in a normal fashion.

By late afternoon they were decorating the tree. Mari watched Lise pull out but then set right back into the box the flags and other decorations with national emblems. There weren't many other choices, unfortunately. All that was left to use were a handful of lace snowflakes, shiny stars, and some colorful balls and birds..

"I know what," Lise said. "I'll start on a paper chain. We won't have any berries to string this year—they all went into the jams."

Lise got to work with the scissors and resumed humming a familiar carol. Mari snapped the lid shut on the box of forbidden decorations, then headed toward the stairs.

"Can you get that into the attic on your own, or do you

need help?" Lise asked.

"I can put them where they belong," Mari called back from the stairs, and slipped into her room.

Chapter Twenty-One

Jul Surprise

In Bestemor's cottage, Odin pressed his back against the hearth wall, stretched, and yawned. Mari added a small log to the fire and stooped to scratch his neck. She gathered her robe and settled herself onto her grandma's sofa, pulling the covers over her lap.

"It feels like forever, doesn't it? How long can someone take to eat a few potatoes and lutefisk?" Mari took great satisfaction in knowing that the German "guest" would be eating the preserved-cod dish without the tasty butter or cream sauce. For dessert she and Lise had used their poor excuse for flour (and no sugar) to make 'traditional' waffles. Those would be served plain, without berries or cream. Mari and Odin had shared the best part of the meal earlier, a hearty soup made with rabbit that Bjorn managed to trap just that morning.

"At least you had a holiday treat, Odin. Bone marrow! The *nisse* must have seen what a good dog you've been this year and led the rabbit to the trap."

Odin's tail smacked the hearth a few times. Then he sighed and his head drooped back to the floor, lids closed.

Mari and Odin had retired to the cottage by late afternoon, even though the visit was scheduled for six o'clock. She was taking no chances in case the German showed up early. No one could guess how long he might stay.

Bjorn shared some local jokes about the visits. Some said the soldiers would turn around and head back to the barracks when they crossed the thresholds and smelled lutefisk. Others said they'd leave when the farting started. Of course some worried the unwanted guests might stay too long, especially if a pretty girl was at the table. Mari noticed Lise rubbing her ring when that was mentioned.

Mari checked the clock, expecting to see both hands pointing to twelve. But it was only half past nine. Why so late? Everyone had hoped the German soldier would be gone by now. She had spent the first few hours completing her secret project, then she tried reading. Nothing really distracted her from thinking about tall black boots under their table, probably at her seat. She pictured a German hand lifting one of Mama's best teacups. The same hand that was raised in a "Heil Hitler" salute during troop marches through the village. The black leather belt and holster at his hip would be within inches of someone in her family.

"*Nei, nei,* you'll catch the flu!" Bestemor's voice rang out in the yard, mingled with the sharp sound of boots on the cobbled path. Mari's stomach twisted into a knot. She quickly stretched out on the sofa, pulled the covers over her shoulder, and settled her head on the pillow. Odin had stood up at the sound of voices and was at her side immediately. She swung her arm around his chest, covering him with the blanket, and forced herself to close her eyes. She slid one hand across his muzzle and willed him to stay quiet. The footsteps arrived outside the door.

"Please, don't. She's been so sick." Bestemor's voice verged on panic.

"I'll just take a quick look around. You should quiet down or you'll be the one to wake her."

Mari heard the knob turn and the door swing open. Someone walked into the room. Odin tensed under her arm and she pretended to wake up, trying to look confused. In the flickering firelight she looked straight down at black boots, then up, up, up into the face of Scarecrow.

"So sorry to wake you, little *Fräulein,* but my orders are to look through all the buildings. Go back to sleep, this won't take long." He took a step toward the back of the house, toward her grandma's bedroom. Odin's low growl caught his attention, and the soldier stopped in his tracks. His eyes searched the sofa and he saw Mari clutching her dog. He turned and approached.

Mari's worst imaginings couldn't equal this—Scarecrow in Bestemor's home! Would he find the radio? Would he hurt Odin again? Her stomach clenched, bile rising in her throat. Just as he reached her side she doubled over and vomited.

"*Mein Godt!*" he shouted, jumping backward. His boots and pants were covered with half-digested rabbit soup.

"I tried to warn you," Bestemor said, making an effort to sound solicitous. "You must get out of those clothes and clean yourself up before you catch what she has."

Scarecrow shook first one leg then the other, muttering to himself. "Yes, yes, that would be best." He hustled out the door and called back. "Please give my thanks to your family for the fine holiday meal." His boots clanked along the stones, followed by the sound of the gate slamming shut.

Mari and her grandma had momentarily frozen. As the sound of crunching gravel faded away, they looked at each other, then the floor, then burst into a fit of giggles.

~

Mari was helping Bestemor clean up when Mama and Papa stepped through the door. At the sight of their confused faces Mari and her grandma broke into giggles again.

Papa scanned the room. "Is he gone? What happened?"

Mama helped Bestemor up from the floor and took over cleaning. The explanation left everyone in a surprisingly cheery state. When they returned to the house and repeated the story, they were all feeling much more festive.

"Are you sure you are well enough to help?" Lise asked Mari with a smile. They stood at the counter preparing their family's "real" holiday treats.

"Of course, I don't have the flu. My stomach just gets upset when I get scared. I've been learning to hold it back, but this time it seemed better to play my part."

They grinned at each other and continued setting up a simple but festive table, including wonderful treats they hadn't seen in months. Mari's mouth watered, and she definitely had an appetite again. Lise's boyfriend Erik's family lived on a farm a good distance away from Oslo, where rationing was less a problem as they could provide for themselves. Lise and Erik had traveled to his home, then she continued on to Ytre Arna—with a suitcase full of cheeses, sausages, lefsa, real breads, and even some honeys and jams.

"Weren't you afraid they would search your luggage?" Mari asked, trying not to drool at the sight of such familiar but now rare foods.

"Actually, I asked a German officer to help me carry the heavier suitcase. I said it was full of books."

Mari's eyes grew wide, marveling at her sister's nerves.

Lise laughed. "I got the idea from one of our professors, an older woman. She said she brought half a gigantic ham back from her brother's farm with the help of soldiers transferring her heavy luggage all along the train route. They are so frustrated by the ice front that when one of us speaks to them or asks for help, they rush to do our bidding." She laid out the last of the small open-faced sandwiches and lit the candles.

Just then Papa entered the room wearing his *bunad*

shirt and vest, the festive dress typical of the region. He looked so grand. Mama appeared next, at his side in her colorful bunad clothes, too.

"Ooh, now we truly can celebrate *God Jul,*" Mari said.

Mama said, "I know it's forbidden, but we decided for just an hour or so, we would risk it. Of course we'll change before we go out to church later. But for now . . ."

Papa nodded, "For now." They walked toward the tree and held out their hands to the family.

Mari said, "Wait, don't start!" and ran out the back door.

In a few moments she was back, carrying a towel. She set it on the sofa and unfolded it. Her family gathered to look over her shoulder as she lifted up one simple ornament after another. Each was made of some scrap of paper or foil in the shape of a ball or a star.

"They're lovely, Mari. Without our flags, the tree does seem bare," Bjorn said.

"But the tree won't be without our flags! Look at this." Mari lifted a small tab on the back of the ornament and it opened like the cover of a book. One of their Norway flag decorations was fastened to the inside. She handed it to Bjorn to add to the tree, and soon everyone was opening and attaching flag decorations.

"We should close them unless we are here, but we must have our *Jul* flags, at least for now," Mari said proudly.

Then, as every year, they circled the tree, clasped

hands, and sang "*Ja, Vi Elsker Dette Landet*," their national anthem:

"Yes, we love this country of ours, as it rises forth,
Rugged and weathered, high above the sea . . ."

Chapter Twenty-Two

Family Time

Mari felt guilty making Bestemor miss the church music and her friends, but she was eager to hear about what happened earlier at the dinner.

"More tea?"

Mari shook her head. Bestemor set the kettle back on the stove and returned to the table. They remained at home while the others went to midnight services.

"Oh, grandma, I never expected Scarecrow to be the soldier sent here! What did Papa say when he opened the door?"

"We each acted exactly as planned. We spoke formally, and as little as possible. The soldier's name is Fritz, and he wanted us to call him that, but no one ever spoke his name."

Mari fiddled with her empty cup, tipping it first one way then the other. "I hope he was miserable! It must have made a very long quiet meal. I thought he would never leave."

Bestemor took the cup from Mari's hands and pushed her chair back. "Come, let's sit where we can see the tree." She wrapped her arm around Mari's shoulder and they made their way to the sofa. She sat at one end and pulled a pillow onto her lap. "Lie down and rest, I'll tell you all about it, if you want to hear."

Mari stretched out on the sofa and laid her head in her grandma's lap. Odin followed and stretched out on the floor beside them, his head on Bestemor's feet. Mari's fingers found his ear at the same time she felt her grandma begin to rub her earlobe.

"When he arrived he made a show of admiring the tree and other decorations, but that was just an excuse to examine every nook and cranny of the room. After that he was full of questions about our customs. He wanted us to sing carols."

"You didn't, did you?" Mari pictured her family having to perform for him like school children.

"Of course not. We made a few excuses, then Sonja hurried us to the table. Each food was served with a little explanation. Bjorn rather enjoyed describing how we make lutefisk by soaking it in lye, serving him an extra large helping. It is a strange dish if you're not used to it, especially without the lovely cream sauce."

Mari grinned. "Did he eat it?"

"He did. Every bite. But it took him quite a while to finish. Since there was no conversation, he did most of the talking. He said our house reminded him of his grandparents' home in the Harz Mountains in central Germany. He spent more than a year in frontline battles, so he was happy to be sent to Norway. According to him, this landscape is similar to the mountain area where he lived with his grandparents. It seems he comes from the land of folktales and the home of the Brothers Grimm.

"He told us about his family. His parents were killed in an accident before the war began, and he has two younger sisters who still live there. He hasn't been back to see them for almost three years."

Mari heard something in Bestemor's voice that confused her. She sat up and searched her face for a clue. "He was trying to make you like him! He was trying to make you let down your guard. He didn't fool you, did he?"

"Mari, just listen." Her grandma's voice had a firmness in it that Mari recognized. "He's a soldier, a German invader, he follows orders from our enemy. All that is true, and nothing he said changes it."

Mari relaxed just a bit and felt her hands unclench.

"But Mari—he's also a person, a boy not much older than Bjorn. Think about that. What if Bjorn had been forced into the army and was gone for years without even a visit home. You have to admit it must be hard on him."

Mari sat up and swung around to face her. "Bjorn would never do the things he did!" She shrugged off her grandma's attempt at a hug and crossed her arms.

"No, Mari, I know he wouldn't. Just remember that

144

it is Hitler who is our enemy, the Nazis and their hateful beliefs. People must always decide for themselves what is right. Some obey him eagerly, but others—well, I think they don't see that they have a choice."

Mari stared at the flags on the tree, her fingers buried in Odin's thick fur.

"He made his choice," she muttered.

~

Mari helped Mama return the good dishes to the cupboard. Their reports of the events at church were astonishing. Soldiers insisted everyone open their coats to enforce the rules against wearing their festive bunad clothes. The few who did were turned away, their names were written down, and they were ordered to report to Nazi headquarters the next morning on Christmas Day. Soldiers even remained in the church throughout the services, but not as worshippers.

She pictured the crowded church with soldiers patrolling. "Pastor Carlsson was so brave," Mari said.

Papa sighed. "He was, and I have no doubt he'll pay a steep price for it, too. Just refusing to read Quisling's proclamation about our 'moral obligation to support our German brothers' was bad enough. But he even gave a prayer for our country and King Haakon VII. That could land him in a prison camp."

The platter nearly slipped through her hands when she heard that. Lise took it from her trembling fingers and put it safely on the shelf. "Perhaps not, Papa," she said. "They demanded cooperation from the teachers, too, and from our professors. When so many refused, they took no action against them."

"No action—yet," Bjorn said. "They continue to make ridiculous rules to intimidate us into cooperation. This rule about not wearing bunad is absurd, yet all those who defied it are facing interrogation and steep fines."

Mama surveyed the kitchen and untied her apron. "Their foolish demands can't go on forever, can they?" It was well past bedtime but Mari sensed they felt as reluctant to end the night as she was.

Lise slipped her arm around Mama's shoulder. "They may try, but we are growing more clever by the day at defying them without risk. Erik and I have attended several weddings where the bride, groom, and family members all wore bunad."

"Really? In Oslo?" Bestemor's surprise set her eyes sparkling. She grinned and added, "We could all wear bunad at your wedding!"

Lise nodded and continued. "It seems their official declaration prohibited displays of national symbols and attire on holidays. It says nothing about weddings! So people have been getting away with that, at least for now."

Mari smiled as she pictured her family on the steps of the church in traditional Arna bunad. It was almost too wonderful to imagine.

Lise looked around at their smiling faces and spoke again. "Here's an even happier thought." She paused for dramatic effect, then continued. "We realized that the Seventeenth of May will be a Saturday this spring. So Erik and I will marry on *Syttende Mai*, our National Constitution Day!"

Mari remembered all the years of parades with everyone in their fancy bunad clothes, contests, singing of national songs and flags flying everywhere, all from life before the invasion. The May 17 fest was the biggest celebration of the year.

Until last year. The Germans did not allow any recognition of Norway's Constitution Day. Two Arna families had defied the order by displaying flags at their doorways. Both were arrested and held in prison for several days, as well as being charged huge fines.

Bjorn swept Lise to the center of the room and began to dance. Bestemor started singing, and everyone joined in. Mari's eyes swung from one face to the next, adding their delight to her own. To see her family all together, laughing and singing, flooded her with joy. For the first time in months she felt safe, whole, deeply and truly happy. *Jul* gifts would be meager and few, but this was the most wonderful present she could have dreamed of.

Chapter Twenty-Three

Bartering Begins

February, 1941

G reta gripped a pine bough with one mittened hand and extended the other to Mari. "You can do it, Mari, I cross here all the time."

"But the ice makes it so slick. What if I slip and break my ankle?" Mari shuffled her boots on the narrow granite path and eyed the rocky ravine below.

"You watched me do it, and I'm here to catch you. Come on, Mari, we have to get to two more stops and make it back before dark." Greta glanced at the sun and horizon to gauge how much time they had left. "Stop looking down and jump! On three—one . . . two . . . THREE!"

Mari leaped. One foot landed, then the other. She laughed and clutched Greta in a hug. "It wasn't as hard as I thought. Let's go."

They made their way up and across the mountain, avoiding trails and approaching cabins cautiously. When Greta heard about Lise's spring wedding, she invited Mari to join her when she "visited cousins" on Saturdays.

Mari's family hoped to barter in the outlying areas for ingredients for the special "*kranse kake*"—the almond ring cake—and other wedding specialties. This wasn't officially forbidden, but if Germans discovered anyone with contraband supplies, even if just unauthorized amounts of sugar, butter, or other ingredients for cooking, it was confiscated.

Greta's connections and contacts were safe, though, she insisted, and she had traveled her hidden routes for months without problem. Crisscrossing the mountains together was even better, she said; it gave the appearance of girlfriends on a Saturday outing, which made them look less suspicious if they encountered soldiers.

"The Gundersons are just ahead. Wait here, and I'll make sure it's clear." Nervously, Mari slipped behind a tree and watched as Greta approached the house. Greta stopped to pet a tethered horse, walked past the woodpile, and paused outside a window. Then, Greta raised her hand to signal all was fine, and Mari hurried to her side.

~

"These are lovely, my dear. It's a shame to let them go." The young woman bounced her baby on one hip and slid her fingers lightly along the edge of the lace tablecloth and napkins. "I have no doubt I'll be able to get quite a few of the items you need in exchange for this. Show me your list of ingredients again." She sat down and began making notes.

Mari turned away, trying not to look at the linens. It was hard to see her family's heirlooms heading for someone else's table. "Could you check off the things you expect to trade for, so I can try for the others at our next stop?" Mama and Bestemor had insisted that Lise would have a truly traditional wedding even if it meant emptying their dowry chests.

For several weeks, Mari had taken pieces into the countryside and launched them on a sea of traders. Each household on Greta's routes was like a safe harbor: *Jossing* papers were delivered, news was exchanged, along with contraband and messages from the mountain fighters. On her return trips, Mari hoped to carry home almonds, sugar, and white flour.

Closer to the date, she'd need butter and eggs, although they were trying to locate a source for eggs near Arna. Bjorn was bartering for wine and making some homemade *aquavit* when he could scrounge up extra potatoes.

Mrs. Gunderson handed Mari her list. "I've heard that trading in Bergen is more like stealing. The Germans turn their backs on the black market to get the things they want for themselves, and they pay well for it. The black-market dealers know how desperate people are becoming and give almost nothing in trade. They'll be the richest people in Norway when this is over. And the loneliest, too."

Greta buttoned her coat and wrapped her scarf over her ears. "It's better to trade in the countryside anyway, even if it takes a few weeks to make the exchanges." She caught Mari's eye. "And your family treasures will be appreciated and cared for here, not sent back to Germany as souvenirs."

Mrs. Gunderson nodded and handed Greta a pouch and a folded cloth. Greta hid the pouch and lifted the cloth. She grinned and showed Mari two heart-shaped waffles. "For you girls. A little something to help on your travels."

Her baby began to fuss. "The sun hangs on a bit longer these days, but darkness drops quickly. You'd better hurry along," young Mrs. Gunderson said. "Someone here is hungry, too."

She kissed the downy blond head resting on her shoulder and walked them to the door. "Safe journey, girls."

~

At the next house, the last, Mari placed two pewter candlesticks on the table—small, but slim and lovely. Each had a graceful neck and head of a swan as the handle.

Mr. Halveson lifted one in each hand, turning them over to see the maker's imprint on the bottom. "Oh, my. These are exquisite. Are you sure you must let them go?" His thumb slid along the gleaming base.

"Papa says so. Can you help us?" Mari forced her eyes away and stared out the window.

"Yes, of course. These may spend the rest of the war

buried in a fruit cellar, but eventually they will grace a Norsk table." He patted her shoulder comfortingly. "At least you know they will not be melted down for gun-metal."

Mari smiled slightly when she heard him say the same words Papa had used while wrapping the candlesticks. He had grown up seeing them on his grandmother's mantle. Papa had tried not to let it show, but Mari had seen the wetness in his eyes when he handed them to her.

"We'll have no trouble getting the things on your list. What is the wedding date?"

Greta handed Mari her hat and they bundled them-selves into their coats. "It's in spring, when Lise and Erik can get home from University. "

The family had agreed it would be best for all to avoid giving a specific date. No one outside the family knew of the plans to wear bunad. Even so, their friends in Arna had been thrilled to hear of the coming wedding and offered to help in any way possible.

"That's good. You'll be back several times before then. We'll send you home with enough ingredients for a tow-ering wedding cake." Mr. Halveson followed them to the door, stopping first to take a small packet from a kitchen drawer. He handed it to Greta and watched closely while she secured it in the hidden pocket inside her backpack.

"On your way, girls." He pointed to the setting sun. "You'll have quite a workout to make it home before dark. You can do it. You're young and healthy, not full of aching joints like mine." He rubbed his hip and chuckled.

They waved good-bye to his silhouette in the doorway and hurried to the treeline. Greta's routes were not identical, but always traced an arc up, around, and back down the mountainside. After this stop they were not more than thirty minutes from Arna. They pushed hard to cut a few minutes off that time and had no breath left for chatter.

Mari drifted into her thoughts, soothed by the steady shushing of their feet through the snow-covered forest floor. Since Christmas she had been so busy she welcomed this quiet and isolation. Mama and Bestemor were in a frenzy of stitching, cleaning, and organizing. Papa and Bjorn were gone even more than before. She traveled with Greta on Saturdays, but that meant extra studying on Sundays. The Year Six exams were coming soon, and Mr. Jensen seemed almost obsessed with teaching history and world affairs along with everything else.

In past years Mari had her own obsession at this time of year—her upcoming birthday. She hadn't thought about it in days, though. She recognized some telltale secretiveness in Mama and Bestemor, but she knew they had so many other things to work on.

Her wish, when she allowed herself to feel it, was to have her old bunad altered to fit in time for the wedding. It was a simpler child's version, much plainer than the adult version, but Mama and Bestemor could work miracles with a needle. Mari had grown several inches taller in the past year, her waist continued to narrow, and some shaping would be needed to make the bodice fit. She wanted so much to be able to wear at least a part of her special dress on Lise's wedding day.

"I'll see you Monday." Greta's cheery wave and farewell at the edge of the village caught her by surprise. The darkness was settling in, and they parted ways. Windows were already covered, and there was just a sliver of a moon. She had to hurry home in the shadows as quietly as possible, hoping not to come across any patrols along the way.

Chapter Twenty-Four

Scarecrow at the Door

Mari closed her book and stretched her neck to the left, then the right. It would be such a relief when the examinations were completed next week. Achieving a high score didn't worry her, at least not much. Schoolwork had always been her safe haven. She learned things easily and took comfort in routine assignments and predictable success. Preparing was exhausting, though. Mr. Jensen insisted on reviewing and expanding everything they had studied for the past six years. Now even Mari was tired of studying.

She pushed her books across the table and rose from her chair. "Papa, would you like some tea?"

He looked up from his own paperwork and nodded, then resumed his planning and budgeting for the wedding.

The kettle had just begun to simmer when they heard a knock at the door. Mari opened it, gasped, and staggered backward into the kitchen.

It was Scarecrow.

"Is your papa here, *Fräulein?*"

Mari couldn't answer. She braced herself on the back of a chair and stared, mouth open.

Papa and the soldier saw each other at the same time.

Papa walked to the door and stepped in front of Mari. "*Ja?* What can I do for you?"

Scarecrow looked straight into Mari's eyes, then back at Papa. "Could you come outside?" he asked in a low voice.

Papa nodded and joined him on the sunlit stoop. The door clicking shut was all it took to shake Mari loose from her panic. She raced to the back bedroom. "Mama, Mama, come quick!"

She and Mama nearly collided in the hallway. "Why, what's the matter?"

"The Germans have come for Papa, they took him outside! We've got to stop them!" Mama grabbed her shoulders, but Mari felt as if her knees would buckle at any moment.

Mama swept her arm around her daughter's waist, turning her toward the kitchen. "Mari. Go upstairs . . ."

Mari ignored her and followed right on Mama's heels into the kitchen. Mama's hand stretched for the knob just as the door swung open.

The look on Papa's face was enough to make Mari fear the worst. "Sonja, come outside with me."

Mari moved to follow but Papa raised his hand. "*Nei.* Stay right here."

She stared after them as the door clicked shut, leaving her on her own. Where was the German taking her parents? She felt a scream rise in her throat but it was as if her lungs had no air, nothing. It felt like the time she toddled as an infant after Bjorn when he jumped off a small pier into the fjord in a shallow spot the youngsters like to swim in. When she slipped under water, she wanted to call to him, but when she opened her mouth water rushed in. Soon after she learned to swim, but that time Mama snatched her up and didn't let her near the water for days.

No one was here to rescue her now. Who would keep her safe from the Germans if they took her parents to prison? Bjorn was on the mountainside with Odin, trading and setting rabbit snares. What about Bestemor? Did the soldier take her, too?

Mari rushed to the sink and peered out the window to her grandma's cottage. Mama and Papa were in the yard, clinging to each other. She could only see Scarecrow's back, his gray-green uniform, shiny black boots and holstered gun. She boosted herself on the edge of the counter and stretched to see past them, to see if Bestemor was with them or not.

Papa spoke to Mama. She moved toward the house, tears streaming down her face. Scarecrow headed toward the gate and Papa followed.

"*Nei*, Papa. *Nei!*" Mari's voice returned as she bolted to the door.

Mama opened it before she reached it and swept Mari

into a hug, nearly crushing her.

"*Nei*, Mama, we can't let them take Papa!"

"Shhh, shhh, listen, please. He's not taking Papa away. He's showing him where Bjorn is."

"Bjorn? Why? What happened to Bjorn?" Mari felt as if she were snowblind, looking in every direction but not recognizing anything safe or familiar. Instead being in a swirling blizzard, she felt blinded by fear and confusion, surrounded by loss no matter where she turned.

Mama pulled her to the table and helped her sit, then slid her own chair close. She wrapped both of Mari's hands in her own and pressed her forehead to them. Mari watched her shoulders lift and fall and heard small sobs.

"Tell me, please, what happened to Bjorn?" Mari's tears were flowing now and she bent over until their heads touched. "Mama, please, tell me."

"Yes, yes, I must." Mama pulled her head up and her hands back, wiping at her eyes and sniffling. "Soldiers were patrolling the mountains. They had reports—someone had told them of English spies making their way to Bergen."

Mari clutched at her stomach and rocked slightly.

"Bjorn was setting snares in the woods when they spotted him. He knows many of the local soldiers because of his work in the bank, but not these men."

Mama pulled out a handkerchief and blew her nose, wiping more tears from her stricken face. Mari gulped back sobs and brushed aside tears with the back of her hand.

"They questioned him, and he had his papers with him. Of course, he didn't have an NS card, so they searched his pack and found several cheeses and a bottle of wine. They accused him of taking supplies to the spies and arrested him."

"*Nei, nei,* didn't he tell them about the wedding?"

"Of course, Mari, but they didn't believe him. They said they were taking him in for interrogation."

Mari cringed at the image of her brother being dragged to headquarters or even the prison camp. "Is he there now? Is that where Papa is going?"

Mama shook her head and reached for Mari's hands again. "*Nei, nei.* Just listen. Bjorn had Odin with him."

Mari heart suddenly grew chill.

Mama continued, "When they put Bjorn in handcuffs, Odin tried to get between the soldiers and Bjorn, barking and growling. Bjorn tried to calm him, but he couldn't with his hands behind his back. Odin kept barking and held his ground."

Everything stopped. Mari shuddered and gasped for breath. Mama dropped her eyes and continued.

"They already had their guns out when The Rat and Scarecrow showed up. They were patrolling again in the hills. Scarecrow tried to tell the other soldiers the cuffs weren't necessary, that they should release Bjorn and let him settle his dog. They argued, and . . ."

Mari slid forward on her chair and grabbed her shoulders. "What, what happened?"

Mama fell forward and pulled Mari to her. "Odin was shot."

Chapter Twenty-Five

Broken Promises

Shot! Mari pushed back from her mother's hug so hard it startled them both. She jumped up and ran to the door.

"Where is he? I'll get Dr. Olsen. Was Bjorn able to stay with him?" She was nearly shouting.

When she swung open the door Papa was on the stoop, reaching for the knob.

"Where's Odin, Papa, I'll bring Dr. Olsen and meet you there."

He said nothing. She stared into Papa's eyes and wanted to shake him. His teeth were clenched, and his face was set like granite.

"Papa!" she nearly screamed. "We haven't much time! Tell me now!"

Her father looked toward the table and she saw her mother's head resting on folded arms, heard her quiet sniffling. When she looked back at her father his face had eased. "What did she tell you?" He spoke so softly Mari barely heard him.

Confused, she glanced at her mother and then back to Papa.

"Odin was shot. We have to hurry, there's no time for this. Is Bjorn with him?"

Papa's head drooped and he covered his face. Mari bounced from one foot to the other, anger taking the place of fear. She would go for the doctor without their help.

Papa took her elbow and led her back inside. She pulled against his hand.

"Stop, Mari. There is no hurry,"

No hurry? Without thinking she shoved both hands against his chest and pushed past him. He pulled her back, gripped her arms, and looked her in the eye.

"Odin is dead."

What? How could that be? She searched his face and saw tears fill his eyes. He held her gaze and nodded. His hands on her arms trembled. What was happening?

Suddenly it was as if the air itself was crushing her. Her throat collapsed, her heart struggled to beat. She felt herself shrinking, flattened, empty.

"*Nei!*" she shrieked. "*Nei! NEI!*" Her fists pounded on her father's chest.

He pulled her to him and slid one hand up, cradling her head against his shoulder. "I'm sorry, little one, it's true."

She had no idea how long she leaned into her father's

162

arms, tears flowing and gasping for breath. At some point her mother joined them in the hug. Eventually Bestemor came in the kitchen and embraced them all.

After a few minutes Mari's grandmother patted their shoulders and took charge. "Come now, there are things we must do. Grief will be here waiting for us when we finish."

Mama released Mari. She felt Papa nod and loosen his grip on her, checking to see if she could stand on her own. He started for the door.

"I'm going to meet Bjorn and we'll move Odin to the picnic glade. The snow has melted there. By the time you reach us, we should have things ready."

He reached for the doorknob, but turned back and hugged Mari once more. Then he held her at arm's length and looked her in the eye. "We brought Odin into your life to help you feel safe and strong. He was a good teacher. Now you are as tall as my shoulder, you help us in so many ways. You need to be strong for him. Show him you've learned from his strength and courage." He kissed the top of her head and left.

Bestemor took her hand. "Sonja will get a blanket we can use. You help me find a few of his favorite toys, *ja?*" They walked through the house, Bestemor gathering tied rags, old bones, and a cloth rabbit in her apron. Mari followed and watched, unable to offer an opinion.

Unable to think.

Unable to do anything but force the air to move in and

out of her lungs. Even at that she wasn't always successful, emitting occasional gasps and hiccups.

"Let's take a look in the yard." Bestemor led her out and they explored his favorite places. Mari saw him everywhere; racing to the gate when she returned from school, playing fetch, snoozing in the shade of the pine on weathered needles in the far corner of the yard.

Her mother closed the kitchen door and joined them. She carried a basket and a quilt. The only furniture Odin was allowed on was Mari's bed. He never challenged that arrangement while they were in the house. Sometimes, though, they would return home and find the quilt that usually covered the sofa on the floor, nested in a corner. Mari pictured him, tolerating a scolding with tail tucked and ears down, then clicking to the wall near the stove. Eventually he would catch her eye and give her what she recognized as a satisfied smile. Remembering, she smiled in spite of her pain.

~

It took more than an hour to reach the glade. Her grandma's leg had fully healed, but she leaned heavily on Mari's arm whenever the slope rose or the path was uneven. Along the way Mama explained that the soldiers had released Bjorn and left him with Odin's body. When they approached the glade, they heard the steady *thunk-thunk-thunk* of shovels on rocky soil.

Mari saw Papa and Bjorn on the south slope overlooking the lake. This small dimple in the mountainside collected sunshine like honey. They were digging near the treeline on the hillside several meters above the lake. She scanned the area for Odin. When she didn't see him she released Bestemor's hand and ran to the grave.

Bjorn dropped his shovel and hurried to meet her, sweeping her into a hug. "I'm so sorry, Mari, so very sorry." He held her close for a moment then leaned back to look at her face. "Odin was brave, but this never should have happened."

She tried to move past him to get to the overturned earth. "Where is he? Where is he?"

Bjorn turned her and led her to a pine.

She saw Odin lying there, nearly hidden in the shadow of the lowest branches, his back to her. She rushed to him and fell to the ground at his side. She reached out to touch him, hesitated, then sunk her hand into the fur of his neck. She slid her hand along his side, pausing at his ribs, hoping to detect even a slight rise and fall. Instead there was a hollowness to his body, an emptiness that matched her own.

She lay down at his side, wrapped her arms around him and pulled him close.

"Odin, Odin, Odin," she murmured, kissing the top of his head.

Suddenly she realized her hand was wet and sticky.

"*NEI! NEI!*" she cried, again and again.

Chapter Twenty-Six

Alone

Mari sat wrapped in Bestemor's arms. She felt smothered by ominous gray clouds, yet the smooth waters reflected a clear blue sky.

Mama was busy with Odin, and the grave was nearly dug. Since Bjorn had half-carried her away from Odin, she felt she'd never move again.

"Mari, come and help me now." She saw her mother spreading the quilt on a flat stretch of grass. "Come, please. We should do this as you think best."

Mari didn't answer, didn't move.

"Help me up, child. We'll go together." Her grandma nudged her to get up and then reached for her hand. Her mother had washed Odin's chest and brushed the burrs and needles from his fur. Bjorn knelt beside him and cradled his limp body in his arms. When he stood, Odin's head slid to one side.

Mari reached to support it, half expecting Odin to

turn and lick her hand. Together they placed his body on the quilt. Mari knelt beside Odin. She ran a finger along his jaw, feeling the scar under his fur. Her fingers rubbed his velvety inner ear.

"We'll need to finish, Mari," Papa said. "It will be dark soon and it will take some time to get home."

She nodded. She knew it was true. She couldn't move.

Her mother was at her side, pulling at the quilt. "I can do this for you, little one."

"No," she said. "I'll do it." She hesitated just long enough to take one long slow breath. Bestemor handed her the basket of toys, and she arranged them under his chin. Then, like swaddling a baby, she folded the quilt around him, tucking securely as she worked. Finally she knelt and kissed his head. When she did, the knotted driftwood stick, his favorite, caught her eye. She took it from the pile of toys and slipped it in her pocket. The last corner of the quilt covered his head and was secured.

"We're ready."

~

The walk home was somber, made even more so by the shadows of dusk. At first no one spoke. As they were nearing home, the others began relating memories of Odin: as a puppy, chasing rabbits in his sleep, doing tricks.

Mari heard them speak, recognized the words, but none of it made sense. It felt as if she needed every ounce of concentration to make one foot follow the other, to keep breathing in and out. Odin's harness hung from one hand,

and the other stroked the driftwood in her pocket. Flashes from the last hours skittered through her mind, replaying moments of panic and searing grief.

By the time they arrived at the kitchen door she felt as if years, not hours, had passed since she heard that knock.

"Go up and try to sleep, little one. You're exhausted." Mama helped her out of the sleeves of her jacket as if she were a toddler. "When supper is ready, I'll bring it up to you."

Mari headed for the stairs without protest. She even climbed a step or two, then stopped suddenly. How could she ever sleep in her bed again without Odin at her side? While he was recovering from his jaw injury, she had slept downstairs until he was able to make it up to her room again. For nearly four years Odin had kept her warm, safe. He had listened to her worries, complaints, and dreams.

She retraced her steps and walked to the sofa in the living room. She stretched out and rested her head on her arm, then reached back for the quilt. The quilt that wasn't there.

She squeezed her wet eyes shut and wondered how many tears someone could shed before they would just shrivel up and disappear.

~

When she opened her eyes, she was utterly confused. Slowly she realized she was on the sofa, on her own pillow, under her own covers. The house was nearly dark, but she heard voices in the kitchen. Her hand dropped to the floor and searched for Odin. In a flash of pain she remembered everything and shoved her hand under the pillow.

In . . . out . . . in . . . out . . . she concentrated on breathing. How long would it be until she could breathe without effort? Would anything in her life ever feel natural again?

Her stomach growled as if on cue, and she surprised herself with a half smile.

When she reached the kitchen she found Bjorn and Bestemor at the table.

"Sit, sit." Her grandma rose remarkably fast and tugged Mari to the table. "I have a plate in the warming oven for you. It's good if you can eat something."

She sat in silence, watching Bjorn pour her some tea and Bestemor bring her supper. "What time is it?" she asked.

Bjorn checked his watch. "A little after one. Mama and Papa went to bed, but they said to wake them if you need them."

"No, they should sleep. They both get up so early for work. You do, too. Why are you still up?"

Her grandma poured herself a cup of tea and sighed. "Bjorn wanted to talk to you if you woke up. The young and the old can survive without sleep, so we kept each other company." She patted Bjorn's shoulder before sitting down to join them. "You, little one, needed sleep more than any of us. Did it help? How are you doing?"

The first few bites of potato and beans had gone down easily, but now her throat was tightening, and swallowing anything seemed impossible. How was she doing? How was she going to do anything ever again?

Bjorn noticed her struggle and covered her hand with his. "Bestemor, you need your sleep, too. You should go to bed."

With one hand on the table and the other on the chair back, Bestemor eased herself up. "My voice would argue with that, but my bones have the last word." She wrapped her coat over her shoulders and came back to the table. She bent to kiss Bjorn's cheek, then stood next to Mari. Their eyes met.

Bestemor spoke in a whisper but with certainty in her voice. "It will take time, but the pain will ease. At my age I've felt it many times. You will survive."

Mari nodded, and she felt a kiss on the top of her head.

Bjorn was at the door to walk grandmother to the cottage.

"Good night, Bestemor. Thank you, for everything."

Mari's fork pushed the food around on her plate. She shouldn't let it go to waste, but swallowing another bite was out of the question. Ever since rationing began it was a daily challenge to have enough to eat, but she always managed to sneak a bite or two to Odin. She pushed the plate out of the way and dropped her head on her arms.

That's how Bjorn found her when he returned.

Chapter Twenty-Seven

Bjorn's Report

She heard the door click and Bjorn's footsteps, but she couldn't summon enough energy to lift her head.

He stood by her side and whispered, "Are you still awake?"

She nodded her head, and he sat next to her, putting his arm across her shoulder.

"I'm so sorry, Mari, so very sorry. I should never have let this happen."

Her head lifted and she spoke through clenched teeth. "YOU didn't shoot Odin, HE did!"

"We should never have been on the mountain today. If I had known they were patrolling, I'd have stayed home." He leaned back in his chair and pressed his fingers to his temples.

She sat up and reached for her tea. "It's not your fault. You can't know everything they do." The tea was cold, but at least it went down. "Scarecrow has wanted to shoot

Odin all along. He hated him, he hates us all."

Bjorn's brow creased and he shook his head. "*Nei,* Mari, it wasn't him. He tried to stop it."

It was Mari's turn to shake her head in denial, but he continued. "I've never met the soldiers who stopped me, never even seen them around town. They were young and belligerent. Even my best 'banker's smile' and reassurances didn't dissuade them. "

He stared at the door as if a scene was playing out on a screen. Mari watched emotions transform his face as he told her what happened that afternoon.

"I was handcuffed at gunpoint and scared out of my wits when Scarecrow and The Rat showed up. I poured on the charm as if we were old friends. But The Rat said, 'I knew he was one of them,' in German. His partner argued with him and wanted them to release me.

"We heard Odin's bark, and The Rat pulled his gun. Scarecrow spread his arms and tried to make the others back up. He picked up the harness and told them to release me so I could control the dog. I said the same and called to Odin, knelt down so he would come to me and not attack.

Mari's hands gripped the table edge so hard they were numb. Taking a breath felt as painful as it must have been for Odin when his ribs were injured. She pictured Scarecrow's boots: kicking him, standing next to Bestemor's sofa, walking through their gate to point the way to Odin's body.

Bjorn's voice dropped away and Mari had to lean closer to hear. "Odin tried to protect me, but I couldn't protect him. He was so brave. Scarecrow came forward with the harness, Odin lunged at his arm, and The Rat shot him."

Mari pushed back her chair and clenched both fists in her lap. "I knew it! Whether he pulled the trigger or not, he's the one who killed him."

"No, he was trying to help, I'm sure of that. After Odin was shot, he demanded that they release me. There was nothing I could do for Odin, but I heard Scarecrow telling them about Lise's wedding. He's the reason they let me stay with Odin."

Mari's face pinched into an angry scowl. She swung her shoulders away from her brother and muttered, "So now he's your friend? He's on *our* side? Did you invite him to the wedding?" She couldn't stand the sound of the words coming out of her brother's mouth.

"*Nei*, of course not. But you should know something else about him. He asked to be matched with our family at *Jul* time, hoping to see you and explain about Odin."

"What? What could he explain?" Mari jumped up from the table and stalked to the sink. She folded her arms across her chest and stared at the blackout curtain on the window. In her mind's eye she saw into the yard, to Bestemor's doorway, saw *him* barging in to search at Christmastime. "You can't believe anything he says."

Her shoulders stiffened and she stepped aside when she felt Bjorn approach.

"He was anxious to see if Odin recovered, Mari. He said he only kicked him to keep The Rat from shooting him."

"And you believed that?" Mari asked with contempt. Her breath caught in her throat; it felt as if she'd been running a race. How could Bjorn be fooled so easily? "What else would you expect him to say?"

Bjorn stepped away from her and set the kettle to heat. She glared out the window, feeling her anger twist every muscle in her body. Bjorn wasn't at fault for Odin getting shot, but how could he defend any of the Germans, especially Scarecrow?

Her mind lingered on the path beyond the gate. In a better, safer world, she traveled up the mountain to the glade where she found Odin waiting. Together they walked, and walked, and walked.

~

"Sit, Mari. Please." Bjorn tugged at her elbow, leading her to the table. Her plate was gone, and two steaming cups of tea were waiting. She sunk onto the chair and reached for her cup.

"You know I hate the occupation as much as you do, and none of the invaders can be trusted for even a moment."

Mari sipped at her tea but refused to look at him.

He cupped his hands around the hot tea and continued. "We can't even trust many of our own people. Quisling's a good example, but he's not the only one. So many others have joined NS. They do it for different reasons and will have to answer for themselves. I don't trust them, but when I see the threats they deal with, I can't judge them.

Mari took another sip. She didn't want to listen, she wanted to return to the sofa and dream of Odin. But she couldn't seem to move.

"The Germans insisted that my boss, Mr. Jonsson, join, and force all of us at the bank to join, too. When he refused, they replaced him as bank president with a loyal NS member. Mr. Jonsson said he was taking his family to live in the north. He claimed he'd work at his brother's factory. I hope by now he's managed to get his family safely across the border into Sweden."

When he lifted his cup she noticed bruises on his wrists and saw his hands tremble. He returned the cup to the table without drinking and dropped his hands to his lap.

"With an NS party leader in charge of the bank now, I don't know how long I can refuse to join and still keep my job."

She glared at him and demanded, "You aren't really thinking about joining, are you?"

"*Nei, nei,* never. But if I had, Odin would be alive now. They wouldn't have searched my bag, they'd have gone on their way, and we'd both be sleeping in our beds." He propped his elbows on the table and held his head.

Mari was stunned. Shocked by the truth of his words. As much as she wanted to have Odin curled at her side in bed, softly snoring, she couldn't stand the thought of Bjorn joining the party. But every word he said was the truth, and she couldn't ignore it.

They sat in silence for several minutes. Finally he lifted his head. "The time will come that I must leave, too, not for Sweden but to join the mountain fighters. My fingers have itched to hold my rifle since the first day the Germans landed on our soil, but never more so than today."

She saw his jaw clench and he swallowed hard. She grabbed his hand. What would she do if he left, too? How soon would it be before everyone she loved would disappear from her life?

He squeezed her hand and turned to face her. "Not now, little one, not yet. But the day will come. I just want you to understand that we all are faced with these kinds of choices, and none are easy. Odin hated his harness, but he learned to accept it because he loved you so much. Staying here and pretending to cooperate with the Germans is like a harness to me. I wear it now to help in the best way I can. When I can no longer wear it without joining the NS, I'll make a different choice."

He caught her eye and attempted a half-hearted smile. "Do you understand?"

She nodded.

"Then try to understand, too, that even the German soldiers have had to make choices. Some wear that uniform proudly and believe every word their *Führer* says.

But some may be wearing a harness they hate as much as Odin hated his. Why they do it . . . is not for us to know."

Chapter Twenty-Eight

It Never Stops

Mari woke without opening her eyes. They were caked and dry, and when she rubbed them they felt puffy. Then she remembered.

"Go back to sleep, Mari." Mama sat in a chair near the sofa. "Bjorn said you stayed up talking half the night. You must be exhausted. Missing one day of school is nothing to worry about with your record."

She swung her feet to the floor and headed to the kitchen. "Year Six tests are this week. I'd rather be there, really. I'll be fine." She poured a cup of tea and sat at the table.

Mama stood behind her and massaged Mari's neck. "I'll send a note to Mr. Jensen. He should know why you're so tired and upset. He might let you take the tests next week."

Mari patted her mother's hands and turned to face her.

"Really, I want to be in school. I'll go wash up and be ready soon."

~

A note wasn't necessary. Mr. Jensen and everyone at school, just like everyone in the village, had heard about Odin. Mari thought that being in her classes would allow her to focus on something else, something painless. Instead everyone she saw wanted to talk about it, to hug her, offer sympathy, or ask questions. It was hardest of all when anyone talked about how wonderful Odin was, how smart, how beautiful.

By noon Mari was tempted to go home. Instead she took her lunch and headed to the far side of the schoolyard. She sat on the steps near the office and pulled the knotted driftwood stick from her pocket. Her fingers traced the gnawed end and her thumb rubbed the weathered wood. Eventually she set it aside and tried to eat her lunch. The coarse bread was hard enough to swallow on the best of days. She found herself choking on the first bite and stuffed it back into her bag.

"If you're not going to eat that, I'll volunteer to help."

Mari's surprise at Astrid's remark doubled when the girl sat down beside Mari and reached out for her sandwich.

"You're welcome to it."

Astrid opened the bag eagerly. "*Takk*, Mari. If I can fill up now, I'll let Mama have some of my share of supper. We never have enough to feel full, but I guess no one does

179

these days." She gnawed at the sandwich and smiled.

Mari realized how lucky her family was to have three incomes, to have three adults able to receive ration cards.

With only her mother to provide for the two of them, Astrid's struggle presented a much greater challenge than what Mari's family faced. Mari watched the slim girl eat and tried to examine her more closely without being obvious.

"Don't," Astrid said. "Don't feel sorry for me."

Mari felt her face flush and she kicked at the gravel. "I . . . I . . . I didn't mean—"

"You don't like it either, do you? That's how they're treating you. When my father died I was only six, but I remember how it felt. Everyone pushing their pity on us, making sad faces and feeling sorry for Mama and me. It didn't help." She looked into the distance, then into Mari's eyes. "Nothing helps."

Astrid's words felt to Mari like a punch in the stomach.

"The pain goes on and on, until you get numb," Astrid continued. "Then it's better—for a while." She shifted on the step and looked directly into Mari's eyes. "Then it's bad again, but never as bad as it was in the beginning. Little by little you get so you can live with it."

"It never stops hurting?" Mari tried to picture Astrid struggling with as much pain she felt, but had trouble imagining Astrid as anything but a typical happy girl. "You must be pretending all the time."

The sandwich sat in Astrid's lap, ignored. "Sometimes, but not often anymore. When I was little I thought that Papa dying was like losing a tooth—it hurt, and there was a terrible sore spot all the time. Then it didn't hurt as much but my mind kept poking at the empty spot, feeling something was missing. For a while I even imagined that he could come back, like a new tooth growing in." She smiled just a little at that.

"But the empty spot will never go away. Even when I have trouble remembering what he looked like, it still hurts, and sometimes I cry. But not most of the time. Most of the time I just do what needs to be done, and—"

Mr. Jensen rang the bell for afternoon classes. Astrid looked at the uneaten sandwich and held it out.

"No," Mari said. "Take it home. And *tusen takk.*" She reached out and squeezed Astrid's hand. Together, they hurried back to join the others.

~

The rest of the week Mari managed to conduct her life in more or less a normal fashion. She took the school tests and felt fairly confident of her success. She helped at home, delivered secret radio messages, and completed homework. Each day after school she hiked to the glade in the hills and spent some time at the graveside talking to Odin. Each night she settled on the couch and stroked the driftwood stick, tears wetting her pillow. Each morning she woke with a salty face, a face Odin wasn't there to lick clean.

Chapter Twenty-Nine

Birthday Surprises

March, 1941

The results of some clever bartering had yielded many of the ingredients for traditional treats, far more than she had imagined would be possible. "I can't wait to show Mama and Papa what we have," Mari said.

Lingering spring daylight allowed her and Greta to walk home from their Saturday outing at a leisurely pace.

"Do you think there's enough you might have a birthday cake?" Greta asked. "That's next week, isn't it?"

Mari smiled at her friend, pleased that she remembered. But she shook her head and then ducked under a pine bough. "Oh, I don't think so. The whole family has sacrificed so much, it should all be used for Lise's wedding. I don't feel like celebrating anyway."

They reached the ravine, and Mari hopped across the narrow granite path that crossed high above it without a second thought.

Greta shifted the pack on her shoulder and followed. "Look at you, little nanny goat! You'll be the last of our class to reach twelve, but I have to admit you are taller now than I am."

Mari grinned at that, stretching to her full height. "I wonder if I'll be taller than Lise when she gets home in a few weeks. I get that from Papa."

Sunshine lasted more than half the day now, and it was shining on Greta's pale yellow hair and bright blue eyes. "But I'd trade an inch or two for your coloring," Mari added. She tossed her head so the end of her dark pigtail flipped forward. Playfully she waved it toward Greta and asked, "Haven't you always longed to be a hazel-eyed brunette?"

They laughed and chattered the rest of the way back. When they parted at the edge of the village, it was still light out. Mari hurried home but no one was there. She left her bounty on the table with a note and headed right out again, climbing up the trail to visit Odin.

~

On the afternoon of her birthday she made a beeline straight home after school. She wanted to have extra time at Odin's grave site before supper. It was four years ago on her eighth birthday when she had first held him in her arms. Ever since then, they'd shared her annual celebration as if it were his birthday, too.

"Mari, do you have a minute?" Mr. Molstad waved to

her from the door of his shop. She couldn't make excuses with him. The shoemaker had been so generous in making Odin's harness. When she tried to return it, he told her to keep it, that she might need it for another dog one day. Mari didn't argue but she knew that would never happen.

"Good afternoon, Mr. Molstad. How are you today?" She stepped inside, and he closed the door.

"I'm fine, my dear. Come, come with me, please." He hung his leather apron on a hook and led the way past his workbench and on up the steps. At the top of the staircase he opened a door to his kitchen. Mrs. Molstad was spooning porridge in the general direction of their baby; the infant swallowed half of each bite and spit back the rest. Mrs. Molstad set the spoon down after every few attempts and wiped his messy face.

Mari grinned at the young child and ran one finger along his downy cheek. "He's so big! And he has your eyes, Mrs. Molstad. He's such a handsome boy."

"Thank you. He'll be a year in June, and he eats more all the time." Mrs. Molstad said, shifting him to her shoulder and patting his back.

A small package wrapped in newspaper was on the counter. Mr. Molstad picked it up and handed it to her.

"Speaking of birthdays, this is for you, Mari."

She tried to refuse, nudging it back toward his calloused hands. "*Takk*, but you've done too much for me already, you shouldn't give me more. Times are so hard now, and you have a family."

Mrs. Molstad said, "We want you to have it, from all of us. Take a look."

They both smiled at her and nodded for her to open the package. It was surprisingly heavy, so she set it on the table and unfolded the wrapping. What she found was a brick-sized slab of granite. Its polished surface was charcoal gray with a slight grain of white along the base. On the face of it was carved: ODIN 1937–1941.

Tears filled her eyes, and she brushed them away with the back of her hand. "*Tusen takk, tusen takk.* It's beautiful."

Mrs. Molstad wiped at her own eyes and said, "My brother Erik made it from scraps at the quarry. Everyone in Arna wants to remember Odin and his sacrifice. We'll all see the marker at the glade and never forget him."

Mari hugged them both and started to wrap it.

"Wait, look here." Mr. Molstad took it from her and turned it upside down. On the bottom was the symbol for Victory and King Haakon—a *V* superimposed with *H7*. "A reminder that Odin stood his ground against the soldiers. And they'll never even know it's there."

Mari felt herself smile and blinked back her tears. "I'm on my way there now. I can never thank you enough for all you've done for me, and for Odin."

~

On her way home from the glade Mari's fingers traced the letters on the marker. She had intended to leave it on his grave, but then worried that someone might pick it up and discover its secret. Bjorn would help her set it into the ground properly on the weekend. And this way she could show her family right away.

She wondered what to expect for her birthday. Rationing was becoming more severe month by month, and the occupation showed no signs of ending soon. In fact, Mr. Jensen's comments and the nightly radio reports made it sound as if Hitler was growing stronger by the day. Nevertheless, she had no doubt they would find some way to make supper special.

That first night Bjorn said he'd get her another puppy for her birthday but she absolutely refused. Since then he hinted several times until she put her foot down and made him promise. She would never have another dog, at least not until the occupation ended. It was hard enough to keep the image of Odin's fate out of her mind without bringing a puppy anywhere near those German boots.

~

Mama and Bestemor cleared away the dishes and refused Mari's help.

"Everything was delicious," she said, patting her waist. "There was so much meat in the stew, it will mean nothing but potatoes and beans the rest of the week."

"Not at all. Spring brings the rabbits out of their holes, and I've been teaching Per to set the snares as well. There's already another rabbit in the root cellar, ready for soup this week."

Mari wondered why Bjorn was spending time with Per. He noticed her puzzled expression. "Per is a very smart boy, but he thinks he knows everything."

Mari laughed and nodded.

"He needs to learn useful skills," Bjorn said. "Providing food in hard times is one, but so is learning the value of silence."

Mari grinned at the thought of Bjorn trying to make Per listen.

Her mother stood beside the table holding a covered platter. Bestemor refilled everyone's cup with real coffee, a splurge that surprised but pleased Mari.

"First, we sing," Mama said.

When they finished she set the platter in front of Mari and removed the cover with a flourish. There was a pile of fluffy buttered waffles, sprinkled with sugar and spices.

"Oh, my—it looks like you used real flour! And butter? Oh, they're too beautiful to eat!" Mari's mouth watered, and she looked from face to face. *"Tusen takk!"*

When the last waffle was gone, Bjorn insisted on running his finger around each plate before it was taken to the sink. Mama disappeared down the hall and returned with a large box. Mari allowed herself to hope that somehow she had found the time and fabric to alter her childhood bunad so she'd have something traditional to wear at Lise's wedding. Mama had been busy, though, letting down hems and taking in waistlines on all her spring dresses. Mari suspected she was using her measurements to work on the bunad, too.

Mama put the box on the table in front of Mari and

beamed at her youngest daughter. When Mama sat down nearby, Mari saw her reach out for the hand of her own mother, Bestemor.

Mari removed the lid and set it aside. She folded back the papers and couldn't believe her eyes. It was a complete adult bunad: embroidered vest, blouse, and long black skirt and shoes. These took months and months to make. Girls her age almost never had something so fine to wear.

She reached out to touch it, checking to see if it was real. "How, Mama, how did you do this?"

"The sewing wasn't hard. Bestemor will explain." Mama's smile filled her face, and she turned to kiss her mother's cheek.

"Bestemor? Did you do this?"

"No, child. My mother made it, many years ago, for my confirmation. Look at the picture."

Mari gently lifted the wonderful fabric and probed in the box and found a faded photo of her grandmother wearing this very bunad. Mari vaguely remembered seeing it on the wall at the cottage.

"She made it so it could be altered as I grew. At least for a while. So Sonja took in all those tucks again that I had let out over the years. Eventually I had to make another bunad for myself, one that could keep growing with me into this old woman's body."

Mama frowned at that and opened her mouth to argue.

Bestemor just laughed. "It's true, and even with rationing I'd never fit in it again. You've grown up this year, Mari. It's time you had a full bunad of your own."

Mari lifted the box and hugged it to her heart, unable to speak.

Chapter Thirty

Wedding Plans

The next morning Mari left for school early. Before bedtime she had talked to her family about her idea and they agreed. She turned away from the main street and shifted the bundle under her arm. There it was, the little gray house on the corner.

Astrid's mother answered the knock. "Mari, is something wrong?"

"*Nei, nei,*" she shook her head and mumbled, unsure what to say now that she was here. "Uh, I wanted to bring . . . I thought you could . . ." She held the bundle out to her. "Bjorn caught more rabbits than we could use, so this one's for you and Astrid."

Mrs. Tomasson's eyebrows lifted, and her mouth dropped open. She found her voice. "It's very kind of you, but you have many mouths to feed at your house. Are you certain?" Astrid was now standing at her mother's side, watching Mari intently.

Mari smiled at Astrid and nodded. "Yes, really. Mama makes a very good rabbit soup, but we've had it so much this year, I feel like my ears are growing." She laughed and pushed the package into Astrid's mother's hands. "Are you ready for school, Astrid? We can walk together."

Mrs. Tomasson took the small bundle from her. "*Tusen takk,* to you and your family. We appreciate it, don't we?" Astrid nodded and smiled. "Get your things and be on your way, girls." She disappeared to carry the package to the kitchen.

On the way to school, they laughed at the surprising idea of Per working with Bjorn. When Astrid asked how she celebrated her birthday, Mari longed to tell her about the bunad, but something held her back. The look on Astrid's face while listening to Mari describe the wonderful plate of waffles was enough to make her feel a little guilty. She quickly changed the subject to Lise's wedding.

It was less than six weeks away and fast becoming the talk of the town. The official invitation list was limited to family, but it sounded as if everyone in the village wanted to come to the ceremony. Her parents talked for hours and hours, wondering how to provide enough food if so many showed up.

They also debated when the actual date should be revealed. Once the villagers heard, it would not be long before the Germans heard, too. What if they put two and two together, realizing it was going to be held on Constitution Day, and tried to stop the event?

~

Per pulled off his red cap as they approached the schoolyard, leaving his overgrown hair looking like thatched hay. He was a full head taller than Mari and bent slightly at the waist, leaning his head forward.

"Well, Mari, you are finally twelve. Are you old enough now to give me a kiss?" He turned his face to the side and tapped his cheek.

Mari and Astrid grinned at each other and rolled their eyes.

"Has my brother been giving you charm lessons, too?" Mari patted his cheek and then ruffled his hair.

He laughed, tried to pat his hair into place, and followed them into school. "Your brother is quite a good teacher, don't you think? In no time I'll have as many girls swooning over me as he does."

The mood at school was considerably lighter now that examinations were over. In recent days, though, many new propaganda posters appeared touting the anniversary of the "glorious Germany-Norway brotherhood." Just twelve months had passed since the Nazi invasion last April, but it felt to Mari like a lifetime.

The shock of those early days had worn off for the Ytre Arna villagers, but not the anger. The hoped-for Allied rescue had failed. Armed resistance from their own forces, the remaining fighters hidden in the mountains, now amounted to little more than skirmishes and subterfuge. Meanwhile, "official" papers proclaimed Norway to be a northern German fortress. The *Jossing* papers reported the presence of hundreds of thousands of occupying German soldiers all across the country, including the elite SS troops, and it seemed to Mari that far too many of them were in Arna.

The day was warm enough for the students to gather for lunch under the maple tree. "Mr. Jensen needs to be more careful next year," Per said. "The little ones love to tell what they hear in school." He took another bite of dark dry bread and gnawed.

Astrid nodded, swallowed. "Every time a door opens when we're in a classroom, I expect to see soldiers march in to arrest him, leaving us with some NS teacher." She shuddered. "Just like Reverend Carlsson and the other ministers were replaced only a few weeks after they refused to read the Nazi proclamation at Christmas."

Greta turned to Mari. "Will Lise and Erik be married in your house or in the church yard?" Reverend Carlsson still held services in individual homes each week for those who now refused to attend church. When the grandpa of one of their classmates, a boy named Kjell, died last month, Reverend Carlsson performed services in the churchyard and led the procession to the cemetery. The Germans either did not know about it in advance or chose not to interfere.

Mari continued chewing her bread even longer than necessary. She had become quite adept at dodging direct questions like these about Lise's wedding. Papa's planning, she knew, included meetings with Reverend Carlsson. The bold idea was that the wedding would take place outside the church, on the church steps, with the wedding party's festive bunad clothes visible to half the village.

"Who knows?" Mari said, still chewing. "I just do what they tell me and wait to hear what's next."

"It's so exciting that you'll be her witness. I wish I had a sister or brother." Astrid folded her bag and tucked it away. "It will be different in secondary school next year. So many more students, all new teachers."

Per swung his arm around her shoulder. "No reason to worry. We'll all be there, we'll look out for each other."

Astrid shrugged his arm away to the sound of laughter. Mari noticed Greta looking from face to face, then gathering her things. Maybe she was thinking the same as Mari. This year they were only a total of eleven students left. How many of the faces would be here again next fall?

Chapter Thirty-One

The Big Day

May 17, 1941

Syttende Mai

"Beautiful, just beautiful!" Mrs. Nilssen wiped her hands on her apron and beamed at the platters of tiny open-faced sandwiches stretched across every flat surface in Bestemor's kitchen. Each was barely a bite-sized bit of actual white bread, with a dab of butter and a morsel of sausage, cheese, or fish, and a sprinkle of herbs. Weeks ago Mrs. Nilssen and her friends had cleared sunny window ledges of geraniums, replacing the flowers with pots to sprout young spring greens to contribute. The group of women had all arrived before dawn to help assemble the food.

"Scoot." Bestemor waved her apron at Mari, herding her past the other women and out the door. "We can finish here. It's time for you to get ready."

Mari stole a glance over her shoulder and grinned. She hurried to the kitchen door and opened it cautiously, worried that she might startle the other women working in there. All week Mama had baked ring after ring of traditional flaky almond pastry, each one slightly larger than the last. Enough eggs, flour, sugar and almonds had been acquired to stack up a full dozen layers, with a light marzipan glaze on each ring. When Mari left to work on the sandwiches, Mama was supervising a team of friends as they assembled the tower of rings.

When Mari stepped into the kitchen, though, Mrs. Tomasson was the only one still there. She brushed back her bangs with her sleeve and looked up. "Isn't it lovely, Mari?"

Mari could only nod in agreement and marvel that ingredients from all across the mountainside had made their way, carried in backpacks across wintry trails by Mari and Greta, Bjorn and Per, and others, to bring together into this masterpiece. Mrs. Tomasson resumed her finishing work, positioning individual almonds on each layer.

"Where's Mama? And the others?"

"Your mother's upstairs helping Lise. The others went home to dress, too. I'll be done here in a minute." She stood back, scrutinized the spacing, then placed another almond. "It's such a shame not to use little flags. Almond cake should have flags."

Mari nodded, picturing other weddings when tiny Norwegian flags circled each ring, with a larger flag

196

proudly on top.

She sighed. At least they would be wearing bunad.

Bunad! Mama had helped her dress in it several times after her birthday, making sure the fit was just right. Then Mama insisted it be left untouched until the wedding. Now, the big day had finally arrived. Mari raced up the stairs.

~

The day was sunny and the weather mild, a nearly perfect spring day in western Norway, with only a delicate breeze drifting in off the fjord. In her woolen long skirt and colorful vest, Mari was very comfortable. As Mari and her family neared the harbor, they could see the white church steeple ahead through the rooftops. When they turned the corner to start up the street, she caught a glimpse of Bjorn and Erik standing on the top church step, craning their necks. Erik was taller than Lise, but stood half a head shorter than her brother. Both looked incredibly handsome and more than a bit nervous.

Mari squeezed Bestemor's arm as they led the family up the hill. Mama and Papa on either side of Lise were just a few steps behind. The street was lined with friends and neighbors, talking and smiling, then pointing at them as they passed. She felt surrounded by a sea of red: jackets, caps, scarves and stockings. Storefronts displayed red backdrops behind their wares. Here and there she noticed bits and pieces of bunad on others: a frilled blouse, an embroidered vest, a bunad tie on a simple shirt.

She felt Bestemor leaning harder on her arm as they slowly climbed the steep side path to the churchyard.

Pastor Carlsson came from around the corner and bowed to Bestemor. "Allow me." He took her grandma's elbow and helped her to the top step. She reached up to hug and kiss first Bjorn, then Erik.

Mari joined them and did the same. When she hugged Bjorn, he whispered in her ear. "You look wonderful, little one."

Mari and Bjorn flanked the couple, with both sets of parents and family members on either side. Each and every person was wearing their finest bunad clothes. The men and boys stood proudly in their fancy vests and jackets. The women and girls all looked just as splendid in their beautiful dresses, with the embroidered bodices, the patterned belts, the polished silver jewelry.

The ceremony lasted only a short time, conducted right there on the steps for all to see and hear. After a brief homily, the vows, and a final blessing, Erik kissed Lise and the crowd cheered. When Mari turned with them to wave, she was astounded at the size of the gathering. Everyone in the village seemed to be there.

Even more astonishing, several were wearing bunad. Mrs. Nilssen waved to her with her lacy apron. Lise and Erik reached the base of the steps where they were swallowed up by a sea of well-wishers.

Mr. Jensen, wearing long white stockings and full bunad, made his way through the crowd and approached

Mama and Papa. "Congratulations!"

He gestured toward the crowds. "I suspect I'm not the only one who arrived without an invitation." He laughed and then leaned forward, dropping his voice. "Even NS members have been lingering at shop doors, eager to get a peek at this glorious event. But perhaps we should move away from the center of town, *ja*?"

Mari had been thinking the same thing. The excitement of preparations, dressing, and the wedding itself obscured any anxiety she might have had about wearing bunad in public. The ceremony was held at noon, a time when soldiers normally were all at the barracks for lunch. But patrols would soon make their way back into town in the afternoon. So the plan had been for the wedding party to return to the house and yard as soon as the ceremony was over. Soldiers were less likely to travel to the outskirts of the village at midday.

Papa nodded, looking somewhat concerned. "We thought some others might join us. But our yard won't hold all these people."

Mr. Jensen nodded, thoughtful. Then his eyes lit up. "I think the school grounds might be the answer, if you agree."

Mr. Jensen made several more suggestions, then climbed back onto the church steps to announce the plans. Then, Mama, Lise, Erik, and Bestemor led the crowd up the hill. Papa, Bjorn, and Mari accompanied Erik's family and volunteers who offered to help to take the trays of food to the schoolyard.

By the time Mari arrived at the school, Mr. Jensen and others had arranged several benches and tables in the yard. She pitched in to help, spreading tablecloths and organizing the platters.

Wherever she looked, it was as if they had stepped back in time, back to the days before the invasion. Shouts from a soccer game reached her from the nearby field. Families stretched out on blankets while babies dozed. Not far from the tables, Dr. Olsen, Mr. Jensen, and several other men had arranged a circle of chairs and were tuning up musical instruments.

Mari started back toward town to see if more was needed from the house. She met Papa and Bjorn transporting the ring cake as if it were a pyramid made of fine china. She shooed admiring little ones out of the way, and they continued the last of their delivery to the accompaniment of oohs and ahhs. Her mother and grandma joined them to make the final table arrangements.

The array of food was astonishing. Mari saw many plates of items she didn't recognize as having been carried there from home.

"So many brought food to share, especially Erik's relatives." Papa took her mother's hand. "Mr. Jensen's request for people to bring their own food was helpful, so there's enough here for everyone to enjoy at least a few bites from the smorgasbord. Mari, go check the house one last time to be sure nothing was left behind. We'll organize and get started here."

Mari was only as far as the post office when she heard loud voices and saw the backs of two soldiers up ahead, talking to a third person she couldn't see. Suddenly the fine embroidery on her vest and the deep pleats of her skirt felt less than wonderful for the first time. She considered slipping between the buildings to return to school by a back route.

Then she recognized Per's voice.

She climbed the steps of the post office, pressed back into the shadows of the doorway and tried to hear what was being said.

". . . troublemaker . . . Constitution Day . . . warning . . . Syttende Mai . . ."

The solders were arguing about something, mostly in German. Mari could only understand a few words.

For once, it seemed, Per was keeping his mouth shut. His head was down, and he was shaking his head a little, in disagreement. Mari saw that he was wearing a black vest and long white stockings, with his pants rolled to just below his knees. He had a blanket over one arm and a soccer ball under the other.

Then, the louder soldier turned slightly, and she saw it was The Rat.

His gun was in his hand, pointed at Per.

Chapter Thirty-Two

Uninvited Guests

Her feet moved in a flash down the steps, and she heard the click of her heels on the cobbles. Her mouth opened before she even knew what she was about to do.

"There you are, Per! The dancing will begin soon, and you're here jabbering away. What kind of a partner are you?" She walked between the soldiers and slipped her hand into the crook of Per's elbow. She pretended to see the gun for the first time.

"What has he done now?" She gestured dismissively toward the gun. "You can put that away. I'll keep an eye on him the rest of the day. I won't let him ruin my sister's wedding with his roaming and foolishness."

She attempted an indignant look at Per and saw his mouth drop open.

He recovered quickly. "That's what I tried to tell you, I'm dressed for a wedding."

"And we're already late, so we'd better get going." Mari pulled insistently at his arm to lead him around the soldiers.

But The Rat had a firm grip on Per's other elbow.

"Not so fast. You're both coming with us. Anyone celebrating Syttende Mai is to be arrested. Norway has a new constitution now. Since the establishment of New Norway, the old constitution is dead. Celebrating it is *verbotten*."

The other soldier, Scarecrow, spoke up. "Wait, I think it's true. Her sister is getting married." He faced Mari, then dropped his eyes slightly. "The wedding is today?"

Mari felt her stomach lurch but forced herself to look directly at him.

"*Ja,* Lise and Erik are home from University. She talked about the plans at *Jul* dinner, remember?"

He nodded slightly, as The Rat looked at him quizzically. Mari continued, "Erik's parents are country people. So we arranged a folk-style celebration, at the school." She felt Per squeeze her hand in the crook of his arm. She gave a tiny squeeze in return, and kept as big a smile on her face as she could manage.

Scarecrow spoke to The Rat in German, confirming what she said. The Rat insisted they should arrest them and take them in for more questioning, but Scarecrow pressed on, reminding him that they had also been instructed to seem to show interest in traditions, like they did at Christmas.

Reluctantly, The Rat put his gun back in the holster.

Mari's stomach twisted and flipped, her throat tightened. Her hand searched for a pocket, for Odin's familiar driftwood stick, but it was at home. Her hand slid to her waist where she touched the pewter buttons on the vest and then smoothed the pleated skirt of her grandma's bunad. She swallowed hard and stood as tall as possible.

"Come see for yourself," she said, and felt Per take a step back. "The food is much better than at Christmas, thanks to Erik's family. We have a real taste of Norway, and music, too. But we're late. Let's go, Per." She tugged at his arm and marched right between the soldiers.

The soldiers continued to argue, but followed them closely up the hill toward school.

Per squeezed her hand again and muttered. "I hope you know what you're doing."

~

As they neared the schoolyard, sounds of laughter and music reached them.

She heard The Rat hiss to his partner, "What did I tell you, this is a Constitution Day celebration! I'll stay here and you go find other patrols. We should arrest them all."

Mari called cheerily over her shoulder, "Families in Norway are very large, you know. Everyone is related. Lise is a favorite of so many in the village, so no one wanted to miss her wedding."

When their approach was noticed, voices dropped and faces turned to stare. Mari saw Papa and Bjorn walk briskly toward them.

204

"Papa, you remember Fritz." She nodded at Scarecrow. Her mouth went dry, but she managed to add, as if it were the most natural thing in the world, "They've come to see a traditional Norsk wedding."

Bjorn reached them first, extending his hand. "Welcome, you'll enjoy this, I'm sure." He shook Scarecrow's hand, but The Rat pulled his hand back to his holster, scowling.

"My daughter and her groom welcome you as well," Papa said, gesturing to the young couple who looked up from greeting friends and relatives in a line near the tables. He and Bjorn carried a bench and set it near the musicians. They had stopped playing, and dancers also paused when the soldiers arrived, wandering off toward the tables of food.

"Enjoy some old-country favorites, while my wife prepares plates for you."

Taking his cue, Mr. Jensen named a familiar tune, tapped his foot, and raised his fiddle. While the music played, the soldiers continued arguing, whispering heatedly to each other. Mari motioned to Per, and the two moved in front of the bench.

"If you sit here, we'll show you several dances, starting with the courtship dance. We call it the *springar.*" Scarecrow moved to the bench and sat, followed reluctantly by The Rat.

Mari curtseyed deeply, and Per bowed at the waist. They performed the familiar dance, spinning and circling.

Mari maintained a wide smile while keeping an eye on them and trying to overhear their conversation.

When the music stopped, there was smattering of applause from all. Mama appeared with two plates, each heaped high with plentiful samples of every treat. She presented one to each of the soldiers and said, "I hope you enjoy these traditional favorites. We wouldn't have any of this, of course, without the contributions from our family from the rural districts."

Scarecrow stood up, nodded politely, and took his plate. "*Danke schön.*" He turned to his partner. "This is a rare treat for us, right, Hans?"

The Rat rose, nodded slightly, and took his plate. "*Danke,*" he mumbled and sat back down.

Mr. Jensen asked, "Per, do you think you could show them the *halling* dance?"

By that time several other students were lingering within earshot and called out, "I can! I can!"

Mr. Jensen handed his hat to Mari, who ran to the edge of the woods. When she returned, Per and the others were twirling and kicking, stomping their heels in time to the driving music. She caught Per's eye and he nodded, waving the others to move aside to the outer edges of the dance circle. Mari hung the hat on the end of a stick and held it out shoulder-high toward Per. He danced a few more steps, then spun suddenly and executed a flip kick that knocked the hat off the stick, sending it flying through the air. Shouts and applause erupted.

"I'm next!" the other boys called. One by one they attempted to do the same, with varying success.

Mari noted that both Germans were grinning and eating during the performance. When their plates were empty, she stepped away from the dance.

"May I get something else for you?" she asked.

Scarecrow rose and took The Rat's plate, handing it to Mari with his own. "No, thank you, *Fräulein*. We have stayed long enough and must return to our patrol in the village. It was an honor to be welcomed at your sister's wedding. Please give her our congratulations."

The Rat stood, straightened his uniform, and clicked his heels. He gave the slightest of nods and started down the hill. Scarecrow started to follow, then turned back.

Mari's throat tightened. She wanted to take a long slow breath, but her lungs felt as tightly bound as Odin's had been when he was wrapped in bandages.

Scarecrow approached her. "We have a dance very much like yours in my country." He looked at the ground and then up into her eyes. "Thank you for a reminder of home."

He swung around and strode down the hill after his partner.

Chapter Thirty-Three

Time to Choose

June, 1941

The festivities continued for several hours, including short speeches by Erik's and Lise's parents, by Bestemor, and more wishes for happiness from friends in town. Bjorn was about to speak when Mari felt a tug on her sleeve. Per was kneeling beside her chair.

"What is it?" she whispered. "Can't it wait?"

"No, come with me." He gestured for her to follow him.

When they reached the far end of the table Per put a finger to his lips. "Just look," he said. He took off his boot, folded down one long white stocking, and tugged at a bit of tape on his ankle. He removed what looked like a thin pencil, but unfurled into a small flag of Norway.

"For the top of the cake," he said, and nudged her back toward the table.

Mari grinned and slid the flag up her sleeve.

Lise and Erik stood next to Pastor Carlsson at the table. He offered a short blessing of their love and their life. Then he added, "How much longer must we wait for a taste of that incredible cake?"

The laughter and applause was just enough distraction for Mari to slip in behind them and add the flag to the top ring. One by one people noticed and as they did, they stood up, silently. One neighbor nudged another, a circle of friends and neighbors gathered around the couple and the cake.

Pastor Carlsson's baritone began, soon joined by the others.

"Ja, Vi Elsker Dette Landet. . . ."

"Yes, we love our country. . . ." It was their national anthem, unheard these days in public, but warmly kept in every Norwegian heart.

Unlike the rousing renditions typical of past Syttende Mai fests, their voices were muted, more like a choir singing a soft lullaby. Only when every verse was complete did they share the cake and gather their things to return home.

~

With the intensity of wedding preparations over, free time was an unfamiliar luxury to Mari. She joined Greta on her Saturday mountain outings several times. It was satisfying to describe the success of the wedding and thank the families who helped make it possible. She even accompanied Bjorn and Per on their mountain expeditions several times and was learning how to set snares.

Before she realized it, the school year ended. This event was marked with a party, as it was every year, including all their families. After the meal Mr. Jensen presented various awards and spoke about each of the students individually.

She would miss him, the only teacher she had ever had. His waist was even thinner than in September, as was his hair. He was so easy to listen to, the rhythms rising and falling with enthusiasm and intensity as he taught, questioned, counseled her class. Even now as he spoke, his humor and energy blended laughter with nostalgia. His voice shifted in tone, though, when he talked about those who were missing, who had left before their final year together. Mari's mind wandered, as it often did, to Sarah and her family, wondering if they were safe, if they had made it to Sweden.

She was startled from her thoughts by Per's voice. He was standing next to his teacher, juggling something quite amazing—an armful of squirming puppy.

"We all miss Odin, but it is hardest for you, Mari. When Papa read in Uncle Otto's letter that their dog had puppies, he offered to go get this one for you."

Mari fought back a combination of astonishment and panic as Per approached, only vaguely aware of the smiles and applause. Her arms automatically wrapped around the furry bundle when Per placed it in her lap.

Mr. Jensen suggested they adjourn to the schoolyard. She released the puppy on the grass and watched it romp with her classmates and their siblings. Bjorn walked up and wrapped an arm around her shoulder.

"Are you all right with this? He's a fine little spitz. His breed also has a long tradition in Norway. He reminds me of Norwegian elkhound, but he'll be smaller than Odin and easier to keep close to home."

Mari shrugged, and her eyes followed the pup. His coat was a fuzzy buff color, with darker tones along his nose and ears. His eyes were nearly black, not brown, but his tail was tightly curled, like Odin's. "I have no choice, do I? He's a wonderful gift, and I should be happy. But it doesn't feel right."

"I think it would be good for you, but it is up to you. You always have a choice, even when it's not an easy one."

She leaned her head against him and knew he was talking about more than this puppy. After a year of occupation, the Nazi's were furious about continued resistance, even about minor things like the ice front and secret papers of jokes and news. Before returning to Oslo, Lise and Erik confirmed that the same was true there. Since *Syttende Mai*, the posters and mandatory NS "information meetings" had increased the pressure to join.

Bjorn had told her he would be leaving for the mountain forces soon.

Per waved to Mari from the crowd on the grass. "Come on!"

"I should go. It really was a very kind thing to do." She joined the circle and sat next to Astrid. The pup was handed around until it reached her lap. He scrambled up her chest and hung on her shoulder for a moment, stole a quick lick at her face, then jumped onto Astrid's lap. There he curled into a tight ball and closed his eyes. Astrid's hands sunk into his fur and massaged his neck.

When he stayed that way for a few minutes Astrid asked, "Would you like him back?"

Mari grinned. "I think he's quite content for the moment."

"Who wants to play soccer?" Leif asked.

A swarm of children of all sizes raced after him to the field, leaving Mari and Astrid alone.

"Isn't he beautiful?" Astrid ran one finger along his forehead between his ears, and he settled even deeper into her lap. "You must be so happy." She turned to look at Mari and seemed to recognize something in her expression.

"After Papa died," she started slowly, "people said that Mama was young and would marry again, that I would have another papa one day. Of course I never wanted another. I'll always have my one and only Papa."

She stroked the pup's forehead while she talked, stealing a glance at Mari once or twice.

Mari rubbed the stick of driftwood in her pocket and nodded. "It was such a nice thing to do, I know they meant well. I didn't want another dog. But now he's here."

"I'll help you with him, if you want." Astrid leaned over and kissed the pup, who roused himself and scrambled into her arms. "He's the sweetest thing I've ever seen."

Mari watched her rock him slightly and heard her humming, She saw herself with Odin on her birthday four years ago, looking just like Astrid did now.

Per ran up and plopped down across from them. Mari put her finger to her lips when he began to speak, and he dropped his voice to a whisper. "Isn't he something? When he got to my house I wanted to keep him for myself, but you need him more." He leaned forward and held a paw between his fingers. "He'll be a really fine dog, and easy to train. He's smart, I can tell!"

Mari had a thought that surprised her. She stood up. "Can I talk to you, Per?"

He sprang up and followed her a short distance.

"First, thank you. He's beautiful, and it was so kind of you and your family."

Per grinned, but as his neck and cheeks reddened, he looked at the ground.

"I had an idea, but I want to know how you feel about it."

His head popped up. "What is it? You never want my advice when we are on the mountain with Bjorn. You never want my advice anytime."

"After Odin was killed, Bjorn wanted to get me a puppy, but I feel I'm not ready. I don't know if I'll ever be ready again."

His forehead creased, and his smile disappeared.

Mari pointed and said, "Look at Astrid."

Her girlfriend was still rocking the puppy in her arms,

her eyes closed.

Mari continued, "She needs a dog more than I do, don't you think? It would be good company—and protection for her and her mother."

She could see Per's face shifting as he considered her suggestion, from surprise, to disappointment, to irritation.

"If you don't want him, I'm keeping him." He started back toward Astrid, but Mari caught his arm.

"But this way, Per, we could both still share him. Astrid doesn't know anything about dogs. And they don't have enough food as it is without trying to feed him, too."

Per relaxed a bit, looking puzzled. "Then why should she have him?"

"She needs someone to love, a dog for all the times her mother is working and leaves her alone. But she needs us, too. We can teach her how to care for him and train him, take them with us on the mountain. She could even learn to set snares to help feed him."

Per considered her arguments. "Well, I asked Papa to bring a pup for me, too, but Mama ruled it out. At least Astrid lives near me, so I could see him all the time."

"Then you agree?"

He nodded. They grinned and hurried to tell Astrid the news.

Chapter Thirty-Four

Another Good-Bye

Per knelt upright and held aloft a very large rabbit. "Look at the size of this one! It must be over three kilos—plenty for Astrid, her mother, and Thor."

Mari agreed and continued checking her line of snares, all still empty. Per had two in his bag so far, and she had only one.

"If my line has no luck, I'll check Bjorn's. Whatever he caught is mine!"

He laughed at her comment and nodded, moving on to his next location. By the time she saw him again at the trail she had one more in her bag, but it was fairly small. But it would do. And she hoped for at least one more from Bjorn's lines.

She set her bag aside, climbed on a large boulder, and unwrapped their lunch. Lard smeared on the dry slabs of bread helped it go down but otherwise did nothing to improve the taste. She had long since learned not to even think about the creamy taste of butter. It only made things worse.

Per reached for his share and gnawed at it hungrily while he paced along the trail, kicked at pebbles, and stared off into the distance.

He stopped chewing and stood facing her. "How soon is he leaving?"

Mari was startled, shocked that Per would know of Bjorn's plans. It was the only thing they talked about at home at night, but no one else was to know about it.

When she didn't answer, he added, "You know, to go to University. It's all he talks about since Lise and Erik were home for the wedding."

"Oh, of course," she said. "I don't know for sure, but probably soon. He wants to take summer classes to catch up. He thinks he should have gone to University sooner instead of working at the bank." She jiggled her feet and rubbed the driftwood stick in her pocket. "I didn't know he talked to you about it."

"We talked more before you started coming to check the snares instead of him," he said, but Mari saw the teasing glint in his eye. "Now I see him just a few evenings a week in the village."

"Don't blame me for that." She gathered her things and slid off the rock. "Ever since spring, he spends most of his free time fishing on the fjord. After last *Jul's* lutefisk supper, Bjorn says it's the one food we know the Germans won't try to confiscate or ration."

Per laughed and took the last bite of his bread.

"We have enough preserved for *lutefisk* to last all winter. Bestemor says between that and all the rabbits, we're becoming a new species—a long-eared cod."

He laughed again and picked up her bag. "I'll carry this for you while you check his lines."

Neither spoke while they picked their way through the trees to the start of Bjorn's string of snares. When they reached the first one Mari knelt to check. "No luck yet."

"I'll miss him." Per said it so softly she may not have been meant to hear, but she did.

When she was back at his side she said, "I'll miss him, too."

~

The next morning Mari walked alongside her family to Astrid's house where Reverend Carlsson was offering services. After he was locked out of the church by the new Nazi-friendly minister, a few families at a time joined him in someone's home on Sundays.

Thor wasn't happy about being tied in the backyard. Off and on he made his feelings known with yips and howls, causing laughter to mix with their prayers and hymns.

The walk home was leisurely, a chance to absorb the sunshine of the warmest day so far that spring. Along the way they stopped to admire the Molstads' baby, who was nearly a year old now and toddling on his own. Mari bent to stroke his silky curls, and he clung to her finger. When she straightened to walk with him, she saw Bjorn take

Mama's hand and squeeze it.

Mrs. Nilssen saw them and waved from her seat on the porch. She worked her way down the stairs and embraced them one after the next. "Let me have another, you handsome man." She reached for another hug from Bjorn, but Papa stepped forward and spread his arms wide, making everyone laugh.

"It's your own fault that you're second best in this beauty contest, Anders," Mrs. Nilssen told him. "You gave your good looks to your son!"

Papa patted Bjorn's broad shoulders and grinned. "That's the price of getting old, *ja?*" He winked at Mrs. Nilssen and kissed her on the cheek.

"Speak for yourself," she said, brushing at her skirt and primping her hair. "I don't plan to get old for a long time yet!"

~

Mari cleared the dinner dishes and set the kettle to heat. When she returned to the table Mama got up and said, "Bring in the good dessert plates and pour the tea, Mari. I'll be right back."

No one was more surprised than Bjorn when Mama returned and stood at his side with a covered platter. "What's this? It's not my birthday."

Her mother set the dish on the table and removed the napkin with a flourish, uncovering a pile of fluffy waffles smeared with butter and sprinkled with sugar. She kissed the top of Bjorn's head and went back to her seat, brushing tears from the corners of her eyes.

"You won't be here on your birthday. Lise won't mind that I held back a few ingredients to make these for you."

"I won't tell her if you don't," he said, laughing. He forked one waffle, then another onto his plate and passed them on to Mari. "Golden treasures like these are harder to find than hen's teeth. Thank you, Mama."

After Bjorn stripped the last drip of butter and crumb of waffle from each plate, Mari and Bestemor finished washing up. Her parents and brother were sitting on the sunny side of the yard just outside the kitchen window. She wiped the table and noticed Mama lift Bjorn's hand to her lips, then hold it with both of hers.

"He's leaving today, isn't he." It was a statement, not a question.

Bestemor moved to her side and wrapped her in a hug. She felt her grandma's fingers rub her ear.

"We were lucky to have him here this long. He has no choice, you understand that?"

Mari pulled back and looked at her grandma. "He has a choice. He's making the right one." She leaned into her grandma's hug and felt her tears flow.

~

"When did you decide it was time?" Mari traced the letters on Odin's marker over and over.

Bjorn looked away from the brilliant lake surface and covered her hand with his. "It's past time, and has been since the Germans first arrived. I should have gone before now. I couldn't go until I knew you were ready."

She pulled her hand away and crossed her arms on her knees. She tipped forward and propped her head on her arms. "I'll never be ready."

Birds called, treetops whistled in the wind.

Neither of them spoke.

Bjorn broke the silence. "You're more ready than you know." He squeezed her shoulder and tugged lightly at her braid. "I wish you could see yourself through my eyes."

Mari sat up.

"You have been through so much this past year, you've shown how strong and smart you are." His finger turned her chin toward him so she was looking directly into his eyes. "Look around at some of our own neighbors who have played puppets to the Germans. *You* know what's right. Bestemor told me what you said this afternoon."

Mari felt for the driftwood stick in her pocket and rubbed, trying not to cry. "Is everything ready?"

Bjorn stood up and reached out to pull Mari to her feet. He swung his arm over her shoulder and pulled her to his side. Together they walked toward the treeline.

"My pack and rifle are hidden near the top of the mountain. I stowed them there last night. If I leave now I'll be there after dusk, and there's a new moon tonight. I should meet my contact before daylight."

They stopped in the shadows and hugged.

"When will I see you again?" Mari lost her battle and brushed away tears.

"When we have our country back. I'll do everything in my power to make that happen." He eased himself from her hug.

"But you will come back? Promise?" Mari knew it was foolish to ask but she couldn't stop herself. She clung to his hands.

Bjorn pressed her hand to his cheek, kissed her forehead, and worked his fingers free. He slung a rucksack over his shoulder. "You know I'll be somewhere in these mountains, doing what I can to reclaim them as our own. Instead of worrying, focus on the day we are all together again. That's what will be in my mind when I think about home."

She stared after him until he was lost in the shadows of the forest.

~

Mari sat beside Odin's marker until the sun edged over the rim of the mountain. Usually she spoke to him, sometimes for hours. Now she had nothing left to say. By the time she reached home she felt exhausted, drained of all her energy.

She stopped at the little cottage to say goodnight to Bestemor. She was surprised but comforted to find Mama and Papa there. She stayed for a cup of tea, wrapped in their laughter as they shared stories of Bjorn in his younger days.

Before long she carried her empty cup to the sink. Bestemor urged her to stay, even invited her to spend the night. She shook her head, hugged each one in turn, and headed home.

When the kitchen door clicked shut behind her she pulled her pillow and covers from the closet. She arranged them on the sofa and headed to her room to change into her nightgown. When she reached the landing, she paused. She pictured the three empty rooms along the upstairs hallway. Lise was gone. Bjorn was gone. Odin was gone. She walked back down the few steps and stood in the hall, looking out beyond the yard to Bestemor's open door.

Mari stared at the sofa for several minutes. One step at a time, slowly, she walked to the couch and bundled the bedding under her arms.

Then she climbed the stairs to sleep in her own bed.

END

Author's Note

I've traveled to Norway twice with a friend. Her father was born in Ytre Arna and lived there until he immigrated to Wisconsin in his teens. While staying with her cousin's family we saw many old photos and met her aunts, uncles, cousins, and their families. Her aunt and uncle spoke about choosing Syttende Mai, Constitution Day, as their wedding day in 1941 and the role it played in defiance of the occupying German army. Her uncle crisscrossed the heavily patrolled mountains throughout the winter to barter and collect the supplies needed for the wedding preparations.

During the remaining years of occupation and oppression, her uncle kept a hidden radio, at great risk to his life. Village residents strolled about in the evenings, as they still do today. Idle chatter provided cover for sharing tidbits of news on the progress of the Allied Forces or of the fate of exiled King Haakon VII.

The story of their wedding date, hidden radio, and bartering inspired elements in this story. The plot, characters, and all other details are fictional. Although some people I met there share names with my fictional characters, those names were chosen to reflect the common local names of the district, not to portray actual individuals or their actions.

You might note my decision to use the boy's name *Bjorn* without the *ø* (an *o* with a slash through it) found in the Norwegian name *Bjørn*. This was to make the name more accessible to English-language young readers (where the form *Bjorn* is found in Norwegian-American families). However, I likewise chose to keep the umlauts in German words like *Fräulein,* to make the words seem more foreign to readers, as it was to the Norwegian characters in the story.

Odin's Promise is entirely a work of fiction, but incorporates details about historic events that occurred during the German occupation of Norway. However, the chronology of a few German rules were altered to support the plot, including the confiscation of radios, which happened later in 1941.

For maps, photos, and other content related to *Odin's Promise,* visit my website:

www.SandyBrehl.com

About Syttende Mai

From border to border, the people of Norway revel in their celebrations. Birthdays, christenings, confirmations, and weddings draw families and friends together, sharing traditional foods, music, and stories. On these occasions many wear their national costumes, handmade dresses and suits (*bunad,* plural: *bunader)* with distinctive patterns representing various districts and regions. From the youngest infants to the oldest grandparents, bunader are worn at every celebration. And everywhere, *everywhere*, the flag of Norway waves proudly.

The same occurs at times of public celebration, like Christmas (*Jul*) and Easter (*Påske*), as well as on national occasions, like Midsummer (the day of midnight sun, summer solstice). *Syttende Mai* ("May 17," Norway's Constitution Day) is the greatest celebration of all.

In Norway, people never forget that their freedom is a hard-won treasure. When their forefathers finally secured independence after centuries of control by Denmark and Sweden, the people of Norway could at long last make their own laws, speak their own language, honor their own king, and fly their own flag.

Syttende Mai is commemorated each year in every community and district, much as the Fourth of July is celebrated in the USA. Food, music, games, parades and contests begin early and last long into lingering sunsets. Everywhere, *everywhere*, flags of Norway wave proudly.

Until 1940. The national day of celebration was barely five weeks after the April 9 invasion by the German's. Forbidding flags, celebrations, and the wearing of bunader on that first occasion was a clear signal that Norway was now being controlled by their enemies.

Glossary

To hear these words spoken by native speakers, you can find websites, such as www.acapela-group.com, where you can choose a language, enter a word, and hear it spoken (by male or female voices).

Norwegian Translation Guide

Bestemor (BEST uh mor)—grandmother. Variations: *Mormor* (mother's mother) or *Farmor* (father's mother).

Bestefar (BEST uh far)—grandfather. Variations include *Morfar* (mother's father) and *Farfar* (father's father).

Bjorn (bee YORN)—in Norwegian, spelled Bjørn.

Bunad (BOO nahd)—traditional clothing from each region in Norway, worn on holidays and special occasions. Most young people receive their first full bunad at the age of fifteen at confirmation. Plural: *bunader* (but "bunad" was used for singular and plural in this story to avoid confusion).

God Jul (guhd YOOL)—"Good Christmas" (Merry Christmas).

Halling (HALL ling)—one of many traditional folk dances from various regions of Norway.

Hund (HOOND)—hound, any type of dog

Ja (YAH)—yes

Ja, Vi Elsker (YAH vee EHL skuhr)—"Yes, We Love . . ." These are the first words of Norway's national anthem. These words are used just as "Oh, Say Can You See" is used to refer to the national anthem in the U.S.

Jossing (YOSS ing)—an expression used by Nazi sympathizers to accuse other Norwegians of being disloyal. It was adopted with pride by those who resisted the occupation. The secret (forbidden) papers with cartoons and other stories against the Germans were called the *Jossing* papers.

Krone (KROH nuh)—a coin, the unit of currency in Norway's economy. During the war, metal was scarce, so paper "coin notes" were used. For the sake of the story, the coin was used instead.

Lefsa (LEFF suh)—a soft, doughy flatbread, not sweet. Often spread with butter, sprinkled with sugar and cinnamon or spread with jelly, then rolled and cut into bite-sized pieces. Lefsa is often made with a potato base, but in western Norway, where Mari lived, it is more often made with a wheat flour base.

Mari (MAH reh)—a Norwegian version of the name Mary.

Marzipan (MAHR zuh pahn)—a blend of ground almond paste and sugar. It can be made thick and cut into pieces of soft candy, or thinned to use as a frosting or glaze.

Nei (NYE)—no

Nei, takk (NYE tock)—no, thank you

Nisse (NISS suh)—small gnomes or similar magical creatures, often seen as Santa's helpers. Some traditions say that Norway is so close to the North Pole that Santa's helpers deliver the Christmas gifts so he can have more time to travel to the rest of the world. Plural: *nisser* (NISS ser).

Norsk (NORSK)—Norwegian

Syttende Mai (SITT uhn duh MAI)—May 17. This is Norway's National Constitution Day, celebrated much in the same way as the 4th of July is celebrated in the U.S.

Takk (TOCK)—thank you

Tante (TAHN teh)—aunt

Tusen Takk (TOO zen tock)—"A thousand thanks" (a phrase used to show gratitude for something very special).

Ytre Arna (EE trah AHR na)—a town in western Norway.

German Translation Guide

Auf Wiedersehen (off VEE der zayn)—good-bye

Danke schön (DAHN kah shayn)—thank you

Dummkopf (DOOM kopf)—a stupid person

Führer (FYOOR er)—leader (refers to Adolph Hitler)

Fräulein (FROU line)—young miss, an unmarried girl

Hund (HOOND)—hound, any type of dog

Mein Godt! (myn GODT)—"My God!" (an expression of shock and dismay).

Verbotten (Ver BOH tuhn)—forbidden

For Further Reading

Other books for young readers about this time and place in history:

The Klipfish Code, by Mary Casanova. A story of Norwegian resistance in World War II, involving a 12-year-old girl. Houghton Mifflin Harcourt (Sandpiper), 2007.

Number the Stars, by Lois Lowry. A story of Danish resistance in 1943, told through the eyes of a 10-year-old girl; winner of a 1990 Newbery Medal. Houghton Mifflin Harcourt (Sandpiper), 1989.

Shadow on the Mountain, by Margi Preus. A story of Norwegian resistance in World War II, featuring a 14-year-old boy. Abrams, 2012.

Snow Treasure, by Marie McSwigan. An exciting classic tale of Norwegian resistance to German occupation in 1940. Scholastic, 1942; re-issued by Puffin Books, 2006.

Books featuring dogs in wartime:

Duke, by Kirby Larson. Scholastic, 2013.

More books about Norwegian history and heritage:

A Brief History of Norway, by John Midgaard. Nye Nikolai Olsens Trykkeri; Kolbotn, Norway, 1989.

Folklore Fights the Nazis: Humor in Occupied Norway, 1940–1945, by Kathleen Stokker. University of Wisconsin Press; Madison, Wisconsin, 1995.

A History of Modern Norway, 1814-1972. by T. K. Derry. Clarendon Press/Oxford University Press; Oxford, England, 1973.

A History of Norway, by Karen Larson. Princeton University Press, for American-Scandinavian Foundation; New York, New York. 1948.

Norwegian History Simplified, by Zinken Hopp. John Grieg Botrykkeri; Bergen, Norway. 1963.

Our Escape from Nazi-Occupied Norway: Norwegian Resistance to Nazism, by Leif Terdal. Trafford Publishing; 2007.

Pimpernel Gold: How Norway Foiled the Nazis, by Dorothy Baden-Powell. St. Martin's Press; New York, 1978.

Reckless Courage: The True Story of a Norwegian Boy Under Nazi Rule, by William Fuller, with Jack Haines. Taber Hall Press; Marion, Massachusetts, 2004.

A Short History of Norway, by T. K. Derry. Ruskin House, George Allen and Unwin, Ltd.; London, 1968.

Skis Against the Atom, by Knut Haukelid. North American Heritage Press; Minot, North Dakota, 1989.

War and Innocence: A Young Girl's Life in Occupied Norway, (1940–1945), by Hanna Aasvik Helmersen. Hara Publishing; Seattle, Washington, 2000.

Acknowledgements

This book was years in the making. What began as a possible picture book transformed to an adult novel, then moved to a back-burner file. Throughout those years I never quite gave up on the lure of it. Joining SCBWI (Society of Children's Book Writers and Illustrators) helped me learn and grow as a writer. The conferences, workshops, and professional resources opened my eyes to new and better approaches toward this story. I urge anyone with interest in writing for children to learn more about your local SCBWI group.

Writing friends Jan Gustafson and Marjorie Pagel read earlier versions and encouraged me to find a way to share it with readers. Sharon Addy and Rachel Grinti read passages of other versions and each suggested it could be rewritten as a middle-grade novel. Thank you both for that wise advice.

Several years ago Jennifer Kovarik, curator, and Laurann Gilbertson, textiles curator, at Vesterheim Norwegian-American Museum read much earlier versions and offered both encouragement and professional advice.

Some major subversions of German war efforts in Norway were featured in a 1965 film, *Heroes of Telemark*. The widespread risks taken by citizens to resist and subvert the occupation are less well known. Reading Kathleen Stokker's scholarly work, *Folklore Fights the Nazis: Humor in Occupied Norway 1941-1945*, helped me find Mari and her voice. The bibliography includes many titles I used to research the effects of Norway's long occupation on daily life.

My critique partners are my first readers, and this was true for Mari's and Odin's early days. These writing sisters helped immeasurably in making this story work. I am grateful every day for all the ways my writing improves through knowing and writing with Jenny Benjamin, Lori Kuhn, Dawn Bersch, and Christa Von Zychlin.

My family is unfailingly supportive of any writing I share with them, never doubting that someday it might be read by the general public. Their encouragement and confidence mean the world to me.

Philip Martin, my editor, read one of the "other" approaches several years ago and offered helpful suggestions and encouragement. When *Odin's Promise* was ready to submit, it had become an entirely new work, one I hoped would be a good match for his press. I couldn't have found a better home for this book, or a greater source of professional advice and support than Phil has been and continues to be.

Above all, though, my heartfelt thanks to friends here and in Norway who hosted me during visits, shared stories, and made Norway feel like my home.

CPSIA information can be obtained at www.ICGtesting.com
Printed in the USA
LVOW07s1325221014

410001LV00001B/6/P

9 781883 953652